Friends Like These

A Joth Proctor Fixer Mystery

Books by James V. Irving

The Joth Proctor Fixer *series*
Friends Like These
Friend of a Friend
Friend of the Court

Friends Like These

A Joth Proctor Fixer Mystery

James V. Irving

SPEAKING VOLUMES, LLC
NAPLES, FLORIDA
2020

Friends like These

Cover design by Hannah Linder

This is a work of fiction. All incidents and characters
are products of the author's imagination. Any
resemblance to persons living or dead is coincidental
and not intended by the author.

ISBN 978-1-64540-337-1

For Cindy, who makes everything possible.

Acknowledgments

Thanks to four English teachers and mentors at Governor Dummer Academy—Elizabeth Baratelli, Chris Martin, John Ogden and Mac Murphy—who got me started; and to my writing professors at the University of Virginia, Anne Freeman, Edward Jones and John Casey who showed me what's important and what's not, both in writing and in life.

Thanks to my agent Nancy Rosenfeld; to my publisher Kurt Mueller, whose provided a steady hand at the tiller; to Patricia Anders for her counsel and advice; and to the creative, energetic voice of my editor, David Tabatsky.

Colleagues and friends Scott Dondershine, Steve Moriarty and Tamar Abrams provided insight and practical advice that I couldn't have done without.

Warm appreciation to my partners and co-workers at Bean, Kinney & Korman for their wit, insight, and store of legal knowledge, indispensable in both of my professions.

Particular thanks to my wife Cindy and daughter Lindsay who put up with my idiosyncrasies on a daily basis.

Chapter One

Riley's Report

"Holly died yesterday."

I was in the shower when I heard my cell phone chime. By force of habit, I stepped into my bedroom, still dripping wet, to check the message.

"Holly died yesterday."

I stared at those three words from Riley, an old acquaintance I rarely heard from anymore. That's all it said, a brief, impersonal blast of news, grim tidings with no explanation of any kind. I sat on the edge of my unmade bed and read the text again, as a variety of possible scenarios bubbled up and played out in my mind.

Holly had been abusing prescription drugs for years, at least since Sully left her, and even longer if you believed his version of the story. I hadn't seen her in five or six years, and it took me a minute or two to calculate her age, which I pegged at 38, just a year older than me. Holly was barely 23 when she married Sully. Our little circle of once-promising young lawyers, businessmen, and significant others had predicted for years that Holly would wear herself out one day. Perhaps she finally had, but why was I hearing the news from Riley?

I turned the phone off.

In good times, Holly's haughty assumption of the queen-bee role tended to isolate the Sullivans as a couple, but when most of Sully's friends abandoned him after his fall from grace, Holly stuck with him. The two of them formed a codependent bond, as if a poison seed had germinated between them when they met. The longer they stayed together, the more it grew, and it seemed as if her continuing loyalty condemned her in his mind, as if it demonstrated a lack of judgment.

This wasn't what I had in mind a few minutes earlier, as I prepared to navigate another day.

I had an office-sharing arrangement with Mitch Tressler, an under-employed real estate lawyer, in a two-story, dingy yellow brick building, just around the corner from the Arlington courthouse. We split the expense of a conference room, a reception area, and the services of Marie, a part-time receptionist and secretary with an inquisitive mind and a sixth sense for phonies.

That morning, I felt something about to go wrong beyond the news of Holly, as if her death foretold something much worse. I said hello to Marie, poured myself a cup of black coffee from the communal pot, and shuttered myself in my office. Flopping into my well-worn leather armchair, I dialed Riley's number.

"What happened?" I said when he finally picked up.

"I tried to call you yesterday . . ."

"What happened, Riley?"

"Looks like a drug overdose," he said, confirming my suspicion. "From what I can tell, they think it was probably accidental."

As he paused, I looked again at the dismal message he had sent and the inconclusiveness of his explanation.

"You know, Joth, I always thought Holly would drink herself to death."

"Yeah, yeah, who found her?"

"The daughter's boyfriend. You remember Sarah?"

"Yeah, sure I do. Pretty girl, but she wasn't exactly standing at the front of the line when they handed out brains and good judgment."

"You've always been a good judge of character," Riley said.

"Only when it doesn't matter. Didn't she move out and move in with Sully?"

"Yeah, she did, just before Christmas," said Riley. "She got her sense of timing from her dad."

I found Riley's cavalier manner offensive.

"There's no good time for something like that," I said. "No good time at all."

"Funny, that's exactly what Paul said."

Paul was Holly's brother and her only sibling. Riley's flippant attitude bothered me. Someone we both knew had just died a tragic death.

"Are you suggesting this was some kind of gesture of revenge?" I said.

"No, Holly was too tough for that. The boyfriend popped in unannounced. At least, that's the story I got. Sarah sent him over to pick up a few things she'd left behind and, well, I don't know. There you are. No more news. He found her on a couch in the living room."

"That can't be easy," I said.

Of course it wasn't easy, but I didn't know what else to say.

"No, for sure not," said Riley. "She'd been dead for a day or two."

I paused as the gruesome image formed in my head of Holly, deteriorating on the living room couch.

"How's Sully taking it?" I said, trying to shake myself out of those images with another slug of coffee.

"He was pretty shaken up. The daughter's a mess."

That news came as no surprise. When Sully left Holly, he had moved temporarily into a property Riley owned. Temporarily turned out to be a long time, though, and he was still there.

"But you know Sully," said Riley, "he just keeps trucking along."

I could picture Riley shrugging his narrow shoulders, as if this were just another day for him, reporting on the soap opera of his friends' lives.

"Anything I can do?" I said.

"I don't think so," said Riley. "I'll keep you posted. Wait a second. There is one thing to keep in mind. Paul's blaming Sully for this."

Paul and I had played lacrosse together at the University of Virginia, and it was that same connection that introduced Sully to Holly. I seldom thought of Paul in that context anymore. Now he was just a slick real-estate developer with expensive appetites and an exalted opinion of himself, a guy not unlike Sully, which may be part of the reason they never got along.

"What do you mean, Paul is 'blaming' Sully?"

"You know what I mean, Joth. That he drove her to it, that kind of thing."

"He'll get over it," I said.

I didn't mean to sound so flip, but I wasn't exactly concerned with Paul's feelings. I heard Riley stifle a burst of laughter.

"You know better than that," he said.

I let his comment pass. Riley was right, but this was no laughing matter, no matter which way you sliced it.

"Sully never divorced her, did he?" I said.

"No," said Riley. "He never got around to it. Like a lot of things with him. Holly always hoped he'd take her back, and I guess he might have flirted with the idea every once in a while."

I tapped the eraser end of a pencil on the face of a legal pad. Then an actual thought occurred to me, which I wasted no time sharing with Riley.

"Who's on the title of Holly's house?"

"She is," said Riley. "At least I assume she is."

"But they were still married."

"Yeah, that's what I heard."

"Heard from who?" I said.

"Paul."

I wanted to let Riley develop that thought, to see what his take might be. I already smelled something wrong and wanted some confirmation.

"So Sully, still being her husband, became full owner of the house the moment she died."

Unless the law's changed since the last time I checked."

"You'd think Sully would have thought of that."

"He probably did," I said. "He's no dummy."

As Riley paused to consider what I'd said, I imagined Paul's usually pugnacious expression now colored with pent-up rage.

"You're right," said Riley. "Paul's not going to like it. Not at all. He and Holly grew up in that house."

"Well, at least you'll get your own house back," I said.

Riley chuckled bitterly, as if he couldn't make up his mind whether he wanted the house or Holly alive.

"You think I'll ever see any of the back rent he owes me?"

Our old friend had barely been dead a day or two, and we were already hashing over financial matters.

"Think of it as a sunk cost," I said. "Another one of those things Sully will never get around to, and you know that's probably true."

"I expected that going in," said Riley. "But that's Sully. People just do things for him. I still don't get it."

"He's an expensive friend, Riley. Keep me posted, huh?"

I hung up the phone, determined to let the news fade away for a while so I could get some work done. I had a matter to attend to with my landlord.

DP Tran was a trim, compact bundle of energy and deceptiveness. He ran a private detective agency and a bail-bonding business right above me on the second floor. DP's casual attitude toward technical rules had gotten him in hot water with the state regulatory commission, resulting in a revocation of his detective's license. He was a reliable asset, however, especially in a world where information was at a premium. Truth be told, I admired DP's dogged and unapologetic willingness to dig for hidden answers, and I looked for opportunities to hand him assignments that fell within a private detective's job description but that didn't require a PI's license.

I found him upstairs, where he was moving with dramatic slowness through some forms of an Asian martial art, which he claimed to have mastered. He swore profanely at my interruption, and eyed me expectantly, as if he could sense I was about to steer him to another source of cash.

As an immigrant, DP had an outsider's chip on his shoulder. Neither of us felt integrated into the local community and this created a bond between us.

"Trial's tomorrow," I said. "You got that document?"

"Gonna cost you."

I rolled my eyes for effect. This was a game we had to play out each time, as if the ritual confirmed that we had formed a good partnership, but one that was purely transactional in nature.

"I understand that," I said. "You always get paid, and you know it."

DP fished around the top of his cluttered desk until he found what he was looking for: a certified copy of a fraud conviction from the Alexandria, Virginia Circuit Court. He was habitually casual about methods and form, but he always produced the goods I needed. I glanced at the paperwork to make sure it was procedurally proper and folded it into my jacket pocket.

"Were you planning to bring it down?"

I asked this with the same exasperation I usually showed him, wanting to remind him who was working for who in our little ongoing battle for control.

"You know I'd get it to you in time," he said. "I always do."

"Right," I said. "What's the rush?"

I spent the rest of the morning working on a shoplifting case set for trial the next day. I'd handled dozens of these cases over the years. It seemed like an open and shut affair, and most of my peers would have quickly pled in return for a compromise on the sentence. Not me. My client had lifted a pair of high-powered binoculars from a birding store while his buddy engaged the proprietor in some small talk about birdseed.

They never got out of the parking lot. But my client's buddy was smart. He wasted no time lawyering up and rolled over on my guy. Some lawyers would try a case like this, but only on a gamble that they'd secure a soft-touch judge who'd hand down a lighter sentence than the deal the prosecutor would offer.

That's how it often worked. Research and witness preparation was all a prologue to the real job, which was knowing the players involved and judging what chances to take. That's what always tickled my curiosity and kept me in the game.

What made this case different was DP, a man who could dig and follow a trail like a bloodhound. My client's buddy was the only witness who could possibly testify against my client, and I now had admissible proof that he'd defrauded a business partner in the past year. Would his testimony alone be enough to convict my guy?

Armed with that surprise for the prosecution, I had a good argument for reasonable doubt. The fact that both of these guys were two-bit crooks was irrelevant. It was the chess match we all were playing that interested me.

Since I had everything ready for the trial and had little else to do, my concentration wandered. I knew the call would come. There was a lot of water under the bridge between Thomas "Sully" Sullivan and me and I knew it would all come spilling forth sooner than later. No matter what his reasoning might be, and in spite of whatever pain he might be feeling from losing Holly, I knew that Sully would try to spin our past to his benefit. He really had been a very able lawyer, and those traits never really leave a man.

It was around eleven when he finally called.

"I'm sorry about Holly," I said, trying to get the preliminaries out of the way.

"Thanks, Joth. Me, too."

"How are the kids?"

"They're fine."

Sully sighed and reconsidered.

"Actually, it's been like a death watch the last few years. Holidays were the worst. It's really taken a toll on the kids. Now they can put it behind 'em, or at least they can pretend to."

Sully's cavalier ability to discount the emotional effects of a tragedy on others was one of his least attractive characteristics, but it had been a key to his legal success. I wanted to give him the benefit of the doubt, but I couldn't help slipping in a little barb at his expense.

"Still can't be easy," I said. "Even for you."

My jab went right over his head.

"I'm all right," he said, and I believed him.

He and Holly hadn't lived together for several years. They had shared some good times—and had two kids—but he'd erased those days from his highly selective memory bank long ago, leaving them in his private dustbin of personal history. Sully was especially good at

11

manipulating old memories, molding them into a convenient form for himself, and he was also good at letting go of negative moments.

"If I can do anything—" I said, not imagining what that might be.

"As a matter of fact, that's why I'm calling you," said Sully. "The police asked me a few questions, run-of-the-mill stuff, but they told me to get a lawyer. So here I am, calling you. What do you suppose that means?"

I understood routine police procedure, but the question chilled me, nonetheless.

"It's what they call an unattended death, so there'll be an inquest."

"Yeah," Sully said, "I get that, but what does it really mean?"

"Sully, you practiced law long enough to know the answer to that."

"Even if it wasn't an accident, it's got nothing to do with me. Anyway, I've got an alibi."

A light went off in my head as I parsed his comment. It always made me anxious whenever I felt an instinct toward action. Suddenly, I saw the outline of a trail I knew I had to follow.

"Do they know exactly when she died?" I said.

"I'm sure they do by now."

"Okay," I said, "okay," and waited for an answer that took a minute to come.

"Maybe I ought to come in and see you," Sully said.

"Maybe you should."

It would take him only 15 minutes to navigate the midday Arlington traffic, so I used the time to straighten up my crowded, untidy office. While Mitch was respectful of our shared space, DP was a natural snoop with the discomforting habit of nosing around our common area. As a result, I kept all my work files and materials in my personal office. Every flat surface, from the windowsills to the top of the bookshelves and my credenza, was crowded with books, periodicals, files, and legal pads. Scrawled research notes were strewn everywhere, and most of these were glazed with a thin veneer of dust.

Not the best first impression, even for someone I knew, like Sully.

I had cultivated the image of an unaffected, streetwise defense lawyer, but Sully hadn't seen my office since my days of grander pretensions. We were older now, and the folly of youth could no longer serve as an excuse.

I quickly asked Marie for a dust rag and worked the place over as fast as I could, tucking stray business cards and old newspapers into the drawers of my credenza, disposing of empty Coke cans and sandwich wrappers, and piling legal pads into a corner of my desk, where they would look undeniably professional and appear crucial to the events of the day.

Then I sat down at my desk and finished my coffee, wondering where the years had gone.

Chapter Two

Sully

First thing I noticed when Sully entered my office was how well he had aged, much better than me. It was late March and somehow he had a tan, which contrasted beautifully with his wavy, silver hair, the only obvious sign of his age.

Sully was a small, dapper man and always elegantly dressed, although upon closer inspection I noticed a missing tassel on one of his well-shined loafers, shiny elbows on the hand-tailored suit, and fraying cuffs on his monogrammed shirt. We shook hands and he flashed the gleaming smile that had been his principal stock in trade when he was a promising young deals lawyer.

He sat down across from my desk without being asked, seemingly glad to be off his feet. I braced myself for what could be an uncomfortable reunion.

"You see much of the old gang?" he asked.

Sully still had that beguiling, boyish grin, but when he spoke, I smelled Altoids on this breath and had to wonder what he was hiding.

"No, they're all on the fast track," I said. "I've missed that train."

"You and me both."

I saw a glint in Sully's eye as he recalled our better days.

"Heather?" he said.

"I bump into her around the courthouse. Hard not to."

Suddenly the room seemed warmer and I made a mental note to get DP to fix the air conditioner.

"Remember Brad Sellers?" I said. "He does transactions for some Google offshoot. Making a fortune."

"I'll bet that spins off some criminal work," he said.

"Not the kind I do, Sully."

"He probably weighs 300 pounds by now."

"More," he said. "A lot more. He might go four bills."

Sully's delighted laugh encouraged me.

"I hear he married some young blond émigré from Eastern Europe," I said.

"She's fattening him up for the slaughter."

Sully's laughter increased.

"Best not to get in the habit of talking about killing spouses."

"Yeah," he said, nodding as he looked away.

That sobered him up pretty quick.

"I heard Dave got into UVA," I said. "Congratulations."

"Yeah, Joth, we're proud. Very proud."

I knew I needed to ask Sully a lot of personal questions, so I used one to pivot the conversation toward something more pertinent.

"Can you afford to send him?"

He shrugged as his eyes drifted over my office furnishings.

"I think so. Loans, grants; these things work out."

For Sully, they always had—until he met George Duggan. He hadn't paid a dime in rent or mortgage payments since his disbarment and had spent those years in two houses much nicer than the one I owned.

"Virginia may be a state school," he said, shrugging his shoulders, "but it's not cheap to put a kid through; I'm telling you. Maybe he'll have to go the community college route for a year or two, but it'll work out."

One thing hadn't changed about Sully: he had never been inclined to worry.

"I'm trying to remember the last time I saw Holly," I said. "Not long after you separated, I guess."

"That was four or five years ago. You wouldn't have recognized her."

"The two of you had a good thing going, Sully."

He shrugged again, this time more philosophically.

"For a while, yeah. Every marriage is good for a while."

"For a while? You had a dozen good years."

Sully shook his head.

"We were miserable long before I left her."

"I don't think you want anybody to hear you talking that way."

He smirked and massaged each elbow with the opposite hand.

"That's why I like you, Joth; you're my compass."

Sully folded one leg over his knee, and I watched it begin to jiggle. It made me wonder what was ticking inside him.

"Do you know why I left her?"

He'd told me before, more than once. Each time it was a slightly different story. I shook my head, knowing I might be getting a new version.

"It was the drugs," he said, with a frank nod, which in Sully's case usually presaged an exaggeration—or something worse.

"Sully, the last time I asked you that question you said it was about a fight over another woman."

"That, too."

"Is that when she started hitting the drugs? After you left?"

He shrugged again, as if it gave him a chance to re-shuffle the deck.

"Nah, she was always into that stuff. Cocaine in the '90s and it went from there."

Sully was a callous guy, but when it came to Holly, I expected a little emotion from him, if only for show.

"Do they know what killed her?"

He nodded sagely and when his leg ceased its distracting flapping, I knew that I'd hit on the issue that had brought him to me.

"Preliminary report is diazepam. That's Valium. Problem is, she didn't have a prescription for Valium."

"I see. But you did."

"Yeah."

He didn't shrug this time. Instead, he looked up, surprised.

"You think they know that?"

"I think they will."

I tossed this idea around in my head, looking for the right words.

"Any chance those were your meds, Sully?"

"Valium's a pretty common commodity."

"For example, could she have gotten access to your medicine cabinet?"

"Probably."

"How would she do that?"

19

"We didn't live together, but we were raising two kids, you know. I'd see her; we'd talk. If she needed something, I'd try to help her."

I thought about that, wondering what he really meant by "help."

"When's the last time you saw her?"

"Last week."

"Did you give her some Valium then?"

Sully looked at me blankly and didn't say anything.

"Give me a dollar," I said.

He knew the ritual. He reached in his wallet, pulled out one of the few bills he had in there and slapped it on the desk.

"Okay, Joth. I've retained you," he said, drily. "It's official. Our conversations are now protected. Just like old times."

"You may have lost your license, Sully, but you didn't go to jail."

His tone altered.

"I know. And that was more than I expected or had a right to expect."

"Yeah."

I took a last shot from my cup of cold coffee. I didn't want to rehash any ugly memories.

"Sully, you still living at Riley's mom's place?"

"Yeah, I'm still there."

"How's the rent situation?"

"I'm a little behind. Not that it's any of your business."

"I heard he was going to ask you to leave."

"Yeah, he did, but he's been saying that all along."

"But now I guess you've got a place to go," I said.

I leaned back and watched for his reaction.

"What difference does that make?"

Sully had a sudden edge to his voice.

"It means you have a motive."

"Motive? Joth, what are you talking about?"

"To kill your wife. You got any other place else to go?"

"No."

"You working?"

"I'm working some," he said grudgingly. "Doing some consulting."

Sully looked around my office contemptuously.

"Not doing much worse than you by the looks of things."

I let that pass. Neither one of us could win that kind of squabble.

"Look at it this way," I said. "You and your kids are about to be on the street. Suddenly, your estranged wife dies of an overdose of prescription drugs—maybe your drugs—and you get the house. Huh? Sounds like a motive to me."

"On paper, maybe."

"Yeah, Sully, and on paper is where it counts."

He sulked and folded his arms across his chest. His mulishness frustrated me, but it would be a valuable trait when the police started asking questions. I thought for a moment, my mind racing to a key detail.

"I assume the body was gone when you got there?"

"I haven't been there."

"Didn't you . . ."

"No, Joth. Her brother got there first. He wouldn't let me in."

"Why not?"

I asked, even though I knew the reason.

"You know why. Paul blames me. He blames me for leaving her. He blames me for her substance abuse. He blames me for everything."

"So how come you're still married to her?"

Sully looked up and studied me carefully, appraising how much I knew and how much he should tell me.

"She had the insurance. I needed it for the kids."

"The kids would have stayed insured if you had divorced her."

I stared hard at him and let the unspoken subtext sink in. If they had divorced, he'd have been the one to lose the insurance coverage. Not pretty.

"Did you have a divorce lawyer?"

"No."

It was an obvious lie, and I let him see by my expression that I knew it.

"How 'bout Holly?"

"I don't know. Probably."

"It's going to come out, Sully; you know that."

"Liz Hillman," he said, naming a member of our old circle of lawyers. Liz was one of the most aggressive and expensive domestic relation litigators in the Arlington Bar. And she'd once been a personal friend of mine.

"She's not one to sit on her hands if her client wants action," I said.

"Exactly. We were trying to work it out right up to the end."

I didn't reply. Instead I stood up, itching to take this further.

"You got a key to the house?"

"I do now. It's my house."

"Let's take a drive, Sully."

He stood up, wet his lips and shoved his hands in his pockets. There was something about my idea that made him uncomfortable. That was why I insisted on it.

Chapter Three

A Valuable Asset

Arlington, Virginia, wedged between the Potomac River and the enormous county of Fairfax, is the smallest county in the United States, a slender seven miles from end to end and progressively more fashionable and exclusive as you drive toward its northern tip.

The house Holly died in was situated on two acres of wooded land about half a mile from the Potomac. Sully and I took my car and drove over in a brooding silence.

When we first entered the Virginia bar years ago, the big national law firms were just beginning to establish themselves in the area. He and I started out as first-year associates at a Chicago-based firm with a local office in nearby Tyson's Corner. Our practice areas were different, but we were assigned adjacent offices, and, before long, we were seen together so regularly that we were sometimes referred to jointly as "Joth Sullivan."

I soon came to realize that the structure of big firms and the churning grind for top dollar clients wasn't for me. I washed out pretty quickly and within a year I was hanging up my shingle outside DP Tran's dingy little building. I made a decent enough living there, handling driving offenses and criminal matters. Sully, on the other hand, seemed bound for bigger things right from the start, getting involved in the mergers and acquisitions that were putting Tyson's Corner on the legal map, and we drifted apart.

Although in jest, Sully had touched on something essential to his nature when he described me as his compass. While I had never seen any sign of malice in him, he had an almost juvenile inability to see financial impropriety in black-and-white terms, as a matter of right and wrong. He trusted in his genial smile and quick wit to explain away his tendency toward petty mischief and rule bending. He also trusted an equally hard-charging young entrepreneur with a get-rich-quick scheme, which became his undoing.

George Duggan and Sully cooked up a complex plan. Duggan purchased distressed residential properties in the affluent Great Falls area, while Sully drafted and filed seemingly legitimate deeds of trust, documenting secondary financing from a company called FreeForm Mortgage.

Here's the catch. FreeForm existed only on paper and Sully was the sole owner.

The plan went swimmingly as long as they were able to quickly remodel and flip the properties, and that depended on a hot real estate market. Inevitably, the market cooled and when that house of cards collapsed, their scheme was over in a hurry.

In the end, a lot of people concluded that Sully wasn't as smart as he thought he was, and that opinion stung him as much as the loss of his license to practice law. But his friends and enemies had drawn the wrong conclusion. Sully had a realistic sense of his own high intellect. His problem was that he didn't credit others with equal intelligence. When the carefully constructed plan began to crumble, Duggan proved himself just a little bit smarter and a whole lot craftier than Sully.

Assuming the role of aggrieved client, he brought an ethics complaint against Sully with the Virginia State Bar, alleging financial improprieties. The bar assigned a bulldog CPA to peel back the layers of the financial onion and everything he inspected had Sully's fingerprints all over it. The bar probe delayed the criminal prosecution and it dissolved as soon as he resigned from the bar.

Looking back, I think he hired me to defend him in the disbarment proceedings because he thought he'd be able to run the defense himself with me there just to sign the pleadings, but it was more complicated than he thought. Although neither Sully nor Duggan ever faced criminal charges, Sully was out of business and just as suddenly unemployed. His disbarment put a chill on our relationship, but in the process, we'd seen and measured each other in full.

There was a bond between us that neither of us shared with any other person. We'd kept in touch through the personal and professional tribulations that Sully faced over the half-decade since he turned in his ticket, but the interpersonal magic had vanished along with his bar license.

I often wondered how all of that professional trouble affected his family life.

After he lost his house, Holly, Sully and the kids moved into the white house just off Glebe Road on Arlington's northern edge, about equidistant from the Potomac and the Fairfax County line. This was the home Holly grew up in and the place where she would end her days. It had been built in the early 1960s, when two-story, brick ramblers lined the streets of Arlington, a bedroom community for federal government workers of modest means. This one, featuring four bedrooms, two baths and a family room, was larger than the familiar north Arlington model of the period but still several steps down from what the Sullivans had grown used to. This part of the county was not yet the prime address it would become when developers started knocking down the ramblers and replacing them with elegant new construction. Still, the address sufficed to allow Sully to uphold the image of affluence that was so critical to his model for professional success.

Ultimately, and with brother Paul's grudging agreement to renounce his interest, Holly inherited the place from her parents, Tom and Helen Saunders. It wasn't too long afterward that Sully left her.

Timing is everything, so they say.

The Saunders property was built on the crest of a short rise. It was constructed of bricks that showed red through chipping white paint that gave it a shabby, genteel, antique feel. Virginia creeper had grown up along the lower section of the house as if it would drag the entire structure back into the earth. Two white columns bearing the last vestiges of yellow police tape supported the building's sole architectural feature: a peaked portico that sheltered the granite stoop. A bow in the asphalt shingles showed the need for a new roof, and he would need to repaint it before putting it on the market—if that's what he had in mind.

None of this would be cheap, I thought as I stood on the curbless road, reflecting on the long and convoluted trip Sully had taken since his early days of success in the law.

It was a pristine late March day, and for the first time I noticed buds on the dogwoods and redbuds. Spring was just around the corner, and it was difficult not to reflect on the potential of developing the lot.

"This is a big lot, Sully."

"Biggest in the neighborhood."

Other than the two ramshackle houses on the other side of the street, there wasn't a building in sight.

"What neighborhood?"

"You know what your problem is, Joth? You lack vision. The vision to picture what something will become."

I rose to the bait and goaded him.

"I'll bet Paul figures he can put three houses up on this spot."

"Somebody will, but it won't be Paul. That's for sure."

"If anybody could do it, it would be your brother-in-law. He knows which palms to grease and more importantly, just how to go about it."

Sully grunted a nonreply and started up the concrete steps two at a time.

"But it doesn't matter," I said, "because he's not getting this place."

At the top of the steps, as Sully fumbled in his pockets for the key, I pulled a shred of yellow tape from one of the columns.

"That was a fast investigation."

"Nothing to it," he said. "It was a simple case."

Maybe. It was a small house and even a death inves-
tigation can be conducted quickly if the evidence is thin.
Watching him fiddle with a ring full of keys, I asked if
Paul had a copy.

"Not anymore. I had the locks changed."

"Who else had keys on the day Holly died?"

"Oh, I don't know who she gave them to. Really, I
have no idea. Half her friends, probably. She was always
taking in strays."

Sully found the key and pushed the door open into
the cool, dark interior. He stood for a moment, as if reflecting on happier days, then stepped inside. I followed
him, wondering at the memories and emotions he must
have been wrestling with, even though he showed so little.

"Maybe one of those strays had something to do with
how she died?" I said.

"Yeah, I already thought of that," he said. "I don't
know how you'd prove it, though, right?"

I figured that was a rhetorical question, so I didn't
offer a guess.

Sully flipped on a light switch. The front door entered onto a foyer, with a short open stairway running up
and down to the different levels. Lost in thought, he
strode down the three steps into the living room on the
right.

All signs of the police investigation had been removed. It was a tidy, middle-class living room with spartan furnishings that might have come from a secondhand shop: a couch with frayed armrests, protected by hand-knit doilies, a small TV and a stereo cabinet, featuring a cassette deck and a turntable. The walls were decorated with metal-framed prints of National Gallery masterpieces.

Sully walked over to the bay window that overlooked the rear of the expansive property. I joined him there and we looked out through the multiple square panes. To the right was a detached wood frame garage and behind it a rusted out swing set that looked like it dated from Holly's youth. An apron of brown grass jutted into the untamed woodland that surrounded the property on three sides. If there were any neighboring houses, they were distant or invisible.

"Sully, how far back does the property extend?"

He slowly stuffed his hands into his pockets and swayed on his toes with the pride of ownership.

"Farther than you can see. About thirty or forty yards into those woods."

A stand of hardwoods with bare limbs and a copse of evergreens flanked the swing set, lending the yard an unspoiled, natural feel.

"It's beautiful," I said.

He nodded.

"There's a path out there."

He pointed vaguely toward the line of evergreens.

"It takes you right down to the river."

The path was not visible and the grass leading down to the tree line seemed as unbroken as a prairie.

"How long did you live here?"

He examined the tops of his shoes, his thoughts seemingly far away.

"Three years, four years, I don't know. Kind of blends together. The kids really loved it, though."

"What kid wouldn't?"

"Yeah, well, it's mine now."

Sully turned away abruptly and took a seat in a leather chair next to the couch where his wife had died and began chewing a nail.

"A lot of history here," I said.

This was my awkward effort to ease a bit more conversation into the moment.

"Too much."

"I understand the boyfriend found her?"

"Sarah's boyfriend. Yeah, Joth, that's what they tell me."

"Tell me about him."

There was a fireplace in front of the chair and Sully toed the hearth.

"Not much to tell. His name is Barry. He's a senior, Sarah's a sophomore. Holly didn't approve. Neither did I, to tell you the truth."

"Where's he going to college?"

"I'm not sure. I'm also not sure he's the college type."

"Trouble?"

He shrugged.

"Got a marijuana bust three days after his eighteenth birthday."

"Does that have anything to do with why the kid's not going to college?"

"Who knows? Couldn't have helped."

"I suppose not."

I wasn't about to assume anything about a teenager and drugs.

With a visible shiver, Sully got up and wandered out of the room and up through the foyer toward the dining room and kitchen. I let him go. I spent the next quarter hour surveying the house, alert for anything that might bear on Holly Sullivan's death, but I found nothing that could help.

The wastebaskets and trash bins were empty; their contents no doubt catalogued somewhere in a police report. The dusty spaces in the medicine cabinets showed that containers and vials had been removed, but nothing else remained. On several door jams, I saw remnants of fingerprint powder.

When I was done, I rejoined Sully in the living room, where he was back in the same chair, sunk in like a tired, middle-aged man. Sadness had settled on his handsome features. He looked like a man reliving a broken decade of a wounded life.

"I'd like to have been in here before the police arrived," I said.

"You and me both."

"What happened?"

He shrugged.

"The boyfriend, Barry; he called Paul."

The armchair Sully sat in was one of a matched pair. I took the other.

"Not you, Sully?"

"He called Paul."

"Why did he do that?"

"I don't know."

"Yes, you do."

Sully scowled at me and looked away.

"We didn't get along, Barry and me, okay?"

I waited for him to continue, as it was pretty clear he had more to say.

"He's screwing my sixteen-year-old daughter."

I let that one sit for a minute. Sully might have been a lightweight scoundrel, but he was still a dad.

"When was the last time you were over here before she died?" I said.

"Couple of weeks."

I nodded and let his comment settle. According to my calculations, his timeframe was already shifting. I leaned forward and dropped my hands between my knees.

"Any chance you gave her any Valium?"

Sully chewed a knuckle and I guessed he was contemplating something—not the content of his answer to my question, but whether he should reveal it to me.

"Sometimes I did. If she needed it. And she usually did."

He glanced up and read my expression, which I was leaving as blank as possible.

"But if I did, it would have been a handful here and a handful there."

"All the same," I said, "they're going to know you had a prescription for Valium."

He took a deep breath and I noticed his face had paled.

"This is a lot to take in, Joth. I'm not really prepared for it."

"Maybe not, but we have work to do, Sully. Do you know what Holly was wearing when they found her?

Sully followed my thoughts precisely.

"Nothing special. Jeans and a sweatshirt. The TV was on. She fell asleep in front of it and never woke up. That's what I think happened. It's the only conclusion anyone could reach, of course, but that's not how Paul sees it."

"Was he by himself? The boyfriend, I mean?"

He shook his head.

"I already thought of that, I mean, come on, but there's no question she was already dead when he found her."

This was the second time I'd offered an alternative theory for Holly's death. First, one of Holly's strays and now the much-resented boyfriend. Sully had already thought of both and discarded them. A guilty man would have kept those balls in the air, and so I was persuaded— for the moment, at least—that he hadn't killed her, at least not intentionally.

"Do they have a time of death?"

"Generally."

"You told me you had an alibi. Don't tell anybody else that. You got that? You don't even know when she died."

Sully turned a baleful glare on me.

"She'd been dead for a couple of days before Barry found her. I don't think they're giving it much thought beyond that."

That was something to take note of, and I wondered if Sully knew it. The police wouldn't worry about time of death, or even cause of death, if they were convinced that it was an accident.

"The police would have gone to the medicine cabinets right away."

"And that's just what I did, Joth. They were empty."

I nodded. The story was shifting again.

"Any chance they might have found one of your recent prescription bottles here?"

"Anything's possible."

Sully stood up abruptly and massaged his hands. He stared at the place where his wife had died; then he turned slowly, and our eyes met.

"You know, Joth, Holly and I were married for sixteen years, 'til the day she died. And we had some good days. Lots of 'em."

I studied Sully, measuring his posture and expression. I'd known him for so long that I instinctively understood that he was playing me, so I questioned what reason he had to do so.

"I remember a lot of those days, Sully."

"And we raised two kids. And now they're without a mother."

"This kind of thing sinks in at different times for different people," I said. "No way to predict something like this."

I wondered whether it had sunk in for him, or if this was a charade for my benefit.

"Yeah, that's right," he said. "You know me, Joth. I got a lot of hard bark, but this is tough. It's tough. It's really tough."

I watched him make his point and concluded that he was just trying to convince both of us that he wasn't an unfeeling heel. Sully had never been a trial lawyer, but I always believed he could have been a great one. His gestures and features communicated gravity and sincerity before he said a single word. He knew how to play a room.

"I need some air," he said. "Let's get out of here.

This was a moment when a lawyer might want to give that dollar back and not know much more, but I was already in and not looking back.

We didn't talk on the drive back and said our good-byes in the parking lot outside my office. Sully looked like he needed a drink, and I expected he was on his way to get one.

"Quick question before you go, Sully. You say the medicine cabinet was empty the first day you dropped by?"

"Yeah."

"When was that?"

"Just after the police left," he said.

Once again, he was contradicting what he'd previously told me.

"They weren't going to let anybody in before they tied that down," he said.

"You checked the powder room off the kitchen, too?"

"Yeah, Joth, checked 'em both carefully. Empty."

"Looking for anything in particular?" I said.

This could be a test he might easily fail if he didn't think first. Apparently, Sully had the same idea.

"A prescription bottle with somebody else's name on it," he said. "Pretty good chance they found one, too, if you ask me. But you know cops. Things like that could disappear if they decide I did it."

"I'm not quite as cynical as you," I said.

"You think I'm in trouble?"

"Honest answer?"

"Of course," he said.

His ambivalence was obvious.

"Yeah, anytime an estranged wife dies unattended and the husband's got a financial stake in it, the prosecutor's going to take a look at it. You know that, Sully."

"But it's just a circumstantial case."

I looked at him for a long moment.

"As far as I can tell."

"Can you fix it?"

"Is that why you came to see me? Somebody to get you off the griddle?"

He ignored my question.

"Aren't you going to ask if I killed her?"

There are some things a defense attorney doesn't always want to know, at least not right away.

"Nothing quite so dramatic, Sully. You must be watching too much TV. But what I do want to know is if you think someone killed her."

"Of course not. It was an accident," he snapped. "What else could it be?"

"Not the boyfriend?"

"No."

He stopped and reconsidered.

"Well, if you think that might work . . ."

"But you think it was an accident?"

"Honest answer: Yeah."

I considered what I knew about Holly.

"She knew a lot about dosages, use of substances."

"She was a substance abuser, Joth. People like that die of accidental overdoses all the time."

After a pause, he asked me the same question as before, as if my answer might have changed.

"Do you think I killed her?"

"No, I don't," I said, giving him the assurance he was after. "But we'll see what Heather thinks."

The Commonwealth Attorney's name made him smile.

"Well, we'll see if you still have the old magic with her. Who knows? This might help you out."

"She's married, Sully."

He turned his palms up and grinned.

"A minor inconvenience."

For all his flaws, and there were many, Sully was among the most perceptive men I knew, at least when he was sober. It was what had made him a much better lawyer than me and a real waste of talent.

"Let's keep in touch," he said.

Sully slapped my shoulder before turning to unlock his car. He was still driving the Saab that had been new at the time of his disbarment, and I often speculated that it had probably been purchased with funds gained from the offense that led to his downfall. He took care of the car, though, and it still looked good. A lot better than my car—or me, for that matter.

As I watched him drive away, I thought about Sully's nearly two decades with Holly. I knew they had shared things I had never shared with any woman. Anything was possible with Sully; no emotional reaction was too strange or unpredictable for him, but I found it odd that it took a second visit to the scene—depending on which story you believed—for him to be truly affected by his wife's death.

I went back to my office and made myself another cup of stale coffee.

Chapter Four

The Bullet-Headed Man

The next day, as I was drinking my mid-afternoon coffee, Marie announced an unexpected visitor. I was staring outside at a hole in the ground across the street from my office, where a red brick building had stood since the Depression. I barely heard her say his name amid the bang and clang of jackhammers and heavy equipment, working a little more each day to make a modern office building rise out of that hole. I'd spent a dozen years looking every Monday through Friday at the squat old building that had previously occupied that space, but now I could hardly recall any of its features.

That was also true of the person whose business card Marie handed me: Paul Saunders.

Paul had developed male pattern baldness at a young age and responded by shaving his large skull long before NBA players had made that style fashionable. He kept it billiard-ball smooth, and not only did it improve his overall appearance; it typified his personality. He went his own way, expected deference, and carried himself at a forward tilt like the talentless battering ram he had been on the lacrosse field at UVA.

Paul had never reached the upper echelon of local real estate developers, but he expected to be treated as if he had, especially by people at my level of moderate achievement. I took a certain relish in making him cool his heels outside my office while I finished the crossword.

A few minutes later, I stepped into the reception area and extended my hand with an offer of condolences. Paul responded with a rote application of the congratulatory goal scoring grip we had shared as college teammates. I knew him as a man who lived uncompromisingly in the present, unamused by the sophomoric tales of youthful hijinks that often pass between us old boys from school whenever we decide to get together. I supposed the handshake routine might have been a necessary nod to the past and a way that allowed him to forget it.

I escorted him into my office and closed the door and watched him drop heavily into the chair his former brother-in-law had occupied the day before. He fixed me with a resentful glare before starting his version of an inquisition.

"You representing Sully?"

"You'll have to talk to Sully about that."

Paul nodded his head. He had a habit of assuming the accuracy of his own assessments, no matter what the answer might be.

"Well, you can do him a favor."

"I'm always happy to do anybody a favor," I said.

"He's got no right to that house."

I'd been expecting this visit. From the moment Marie announced his name, I knew this was why he'd come. I wasn't surprised, either, that he showed up this fast.

"As I understand it," I said, "Sully's name is on the deed."

Paul's face reddened.

"He's on the deed because we took care of him when he was down. The idea was, he could live there until he and Holly turned it around."

"They were married, Paul. It became his house the moment she died."

"That's a . . ."

"I know what it is," I said impatiently "It's the law."

I'd had enough of his imperiousness.

"You had creditors after you and you wanted to insulate the property from them, so you agreed that when your parents died it would go to Holly. People pay prices for strategies like that."

"I want that house back."

He sounded obstinate, like a bully on a playground who wants his ball back.

"Yeah, I hear you, Paul. I want to pitch for the Nationals."

"People don't talk to me like that."

"I do. I remember when you were a snotty-nosed walk-on fetching Cokes for your betters."

"This is funny to you, huh? Well, you're making a mistake, Joth."

I paused a moment to allow our tempers to cool, then softened my tone.

"Look Paul, this isn't about judgment or discretion. There's no decision to be made. Sully owns the house and there's nothing you can do about it."

He grimaced.

"I'm the executor of Holly's estate."

"Not 'til you qualify in court."

"Anything belonging to Holly, I mean anything found in the house is owned by her estate."

He was on firm ground now, so I waited.

"It all belongs to her estate," he said, "and I've got to make a precise accounting to the court."

"All right."

"I want the stuff that Sully took."

"Such as what?"

"Look, you may not like this subject, Joth, but you're going to like it a lot less when Heather Burke starts asking about it."

Paul looked at me carefully to see if Heather's name would shake me. Today, she was merely a distraction.

"You're not making any sense, Paul."

That was true, unless he assumed that Sully had had actually taken something from the property. If that was the case, this could get complicated fast.

"If she asks you about the stuff in the house, you've already got a problem. Do yourself a favor, Joth. You tell Sully to put it back, no questions asked, and you'll have one less thing to worry about."

He paused to resettle himself in the chair and then his thin lips turned up in a tiny, self-satisfied grin.

"Anything in particular you can't find?" I said.

"For one thing, there was a laptop that belonged to Holly that I know for sure was in the house the day before she died."

He rocked back in the chair with his big hands on his thighs.

"So you see the problem, don't you? Heather might think that Holly was killed by somebody who wanted the laptop."

"Nobody thinks she was killed."

"I do. And I'm betting that laptop proves it. That's why Sully took it."

"That's preposterous," I said.

I started shuffling some papers on my desk as a way of dismissing his suggestion.

"Is it?" he said, seeing right through my move.

"What could be on the laptop that could concern Sully?"

"Well, Joth, we won't know until we find it, will we?"

"What if Heather decides you've got it?"

My question surprised him.

"She's got no reason to think that."

"You were the first one Barry called, right? You were in there before the police. If it's gone, you probably took it."

"Don't try to muddy the facts, Joth."

"There aren't any facts here, Paul; just wild allegations."

I shuffled a few more papers to let that sink in.

"I'll tell you what, Paul. You qualify as executor. Then we'll talk about it. If you don't, you'll be the one answering Heather's questions."

Paul stood up abruptly.

"They'll be the same questions Sully's gonna have to answer. He had a key and he was there."

He started toward the door and stopped, turning back toward me.

"You've always been pretty straight with me, Joth. I'll give you twenty-four hours to make this right."

He looked at his watch.

"It's three o'clock. If I don't have that laptop by tomorrow this time, I'm going straight to Heather's office."

"Paul."

The sound of me snapping his name stopped him in his tracks.

"What do you really want?"

He nodded at me.

"All right, Joth. I want the property. It's rightfully mine."

"You get the property and the laptop's no longer an issue, is that it?"

He turned his eyes toward a corner of the ceiling panel.

"Yeah, I think so," he said, trying to sound magnanimous. "I'll keep it in mind."

I leaned back in my chair and observed his dramatic exit. Then I gave him five minutes to make sure he was gone and called Sully. He was at home.

I asked him a question he already answered in several different ways.

"When was the last time you were in your wife's house before the police found her body?"

"I don't know, Joth. A week."

"You better get your story straight before someone else starts asking."

"Why does it matter?"

"Because your brother-in-law was just here. He says Holly's laptop is missing."

There was a pause and I heard him wetting his lips.

"What laptop?"

"I was about to ask you that."

"Look, I don't even know if she owned a laptop."

"Sully, any chance you were in her house on the day she died? Or the day after?"

"Don't be ridiculous."

"I think you were in there after she died and before the police got there, and if you're not careful everybody else will, too. Did you take a laptop?"

"I don't like the question."

"You're not supposed to like it, Sully. And it's not about whether you like it or not. You'll like it a lot less if you have some cop coming around to ask you tomorrow."

"Really?"

"That's the threat."

"Okay,"

Sully cleared his throat with an effort and sighed.

"I was in there the day she died. Or the day they say she died. I saw her on the couch and thought she'd passed out. She wasn't dead when I left."

"Then why'd you search the medicine cabinets?"

There was a pause.

"The stuff is dangerous. I wanted to cut off her access. Some of those prescription bottles had my name on them. Come on, Joth. Do you really think I found a laptop lying around and took it?"

"You sure she wasn't dead?"

"Positive. She was breathing. I was married to her. You know how many times I've seen Holly passed out?"

I took in some air and another sip of coffee and decided to let it go until another day. These things take time to come to the surface.

"Look, Sully, Paul just wants the house."

"No kidding."

"Maybe it makes sense for you to work something out before he starts talking to someone else."

"Someone like?"

"Someone like Heather Burke."

"Did he say that?"

"As a matter of fact, he did."

"Did you tell him he has risk, too?"

"What kind of risk?" I said.

51

"Nobody wants this petty mudslinging to go public. At least I don't."

"Maybe I better go see Heather."

"Any excuse to see her again, huh?"

I hung up the phone and stared outside again.

Nothing stays the same.

Chapter Five

The Woman Who Calls the Shots

At eight sharp the following morning, dressed in a conservative gray suit, white shirt, and appropriate rep tie, I presented myself to Betty, the receptionist at the Arlington Commonwealth Attorney's office. Located on the sixth floor of a high-rise courthouse building, it sits across a plaza from its architectural twin, the modern, multi-story jail, where Sully once spent a couple of extremely hard nights.

It was misdemeanor day. All the deputy prosecutors had been assigned to courtrooms, and I knew Heather would be doing paperwork in her office. I'd known Betty longer than I'd known Heather, and she gave me a confidential wink as she announced me over the intercom. I was quickly admitted to the inner sanctum.

Heather's two conference chairs were upholstered in crimson brocade. The fabric of the one closest to the window had faded in the sun and I took a seat there, across from her glass and chrome desk. Her hair had been strawberry blonde when I'd first met her, and with the aid of an artful beautician, it still was. After all these years, she remained slender and shapely beneath the severe pantsuit she often affected at work.

"I figured you'd stop dressing like a man after you got elected to the top job."

It was the wrong thing to say and I saw it immediately on her face, but it didn't affect her congeniality.

"This is still Virginia, Joth. Traditions die hard. A lot of people still don't like women in positions of authority."

I had a sophomoric retort to that observation, but I wisely let it go.

"That's the truth," I said, fiddling with a loose cuff button on my coat.

Heather and I met as young lawyers, when she was a raw prosecutor and I was defending misdemeanors and DWIs in district court. From her first days on the job, she'd displayed a real knack for connecting with jurors and witnesses, which is the hallmark of a top-flight litigator. She'd also developed an ability to get along with men, although she'd always maintained a private and above-board personal life, as I knew firsthand.

She now had a corner office with a view of the Potomac River and the Capitol beyond it. She gave me an amiable smile, but Heather's eyes told me she didn't have time to waste.

"Is this business or pleasure?" she said.

"Any time I see you, it's a pleasure, Heather."

A smile wrinkled her even, Scandinavian features.

"So it's business," she said. "Okay."

Although Heather was a year younger than me, there was nothing in her smooth complexion or animated features to give that secret away. My hair had long gone gray, and I didn't bother to do anything about it. While I was still trim, I knew my face showed the ravages of the years in a way hers did not.

She fixed me with an expression that somehow combined insight and good humor, something she was particularly good at doing.

"I don't see you around the courthouse much anymore. I was beginning to think you were out of the criminal law business."

I winced for her benefit.

"Maybe not."

On the walk over, I thought about how to play this, about how much I should tell her. I could certainly count on Heather's discretion at a personal level, but not where her professional judgment was involved. I knew there were already enough questions, enough loose ends, enough evidence for a deputy prosecutor to convene a grand jury if Paul started making noise, and I wasn't going to stop that process or even slow it down if I played games with her. Plus, there was too much history between us for that.

"I'm here about Holly Sullivan."

"Let me guess, Joth. You represent Sully?"

"You act like you were expecting me."

She showed me a narrow, conciliatory smile.

"I was very sorry to hear about her death. I liked Holly. We all did. How's Sully taking it?"

"It's been tough on him. They were divorced—well, almost—but still raising two kids together. He handled it well, I think. Very civil."

Heather carefully selected a Washington Monument paperweight from the collection of knickknacks on her desk and studied it carefully. Then she placed it decisively on top of another stack of papers.

"You guys started out together at the Regan firm, as I recall."

"You've got a good memory."

"It's part of my job."

"Mine too," I said.

Heather looked at me, as if she were waiting for another shoe to drop. I filled the silence by glancing around. The room was at least twice the size of my office and was as tidy and well-organized as the woman who occupied it. I reflected, not for the first time, that the constantly disorganized state of my house and my life might have been part of the reason Heather had rejected me long ago.

"You look like you could use a cup of coffee," she said.

"Sure."

"Cream and sugar, as I remember?"

I confirmed this, and she picked up the phone and relayed the request to Betty.

I spoke up as we waited.

"It's been a while since you made me a cup of coffee."

"I remember that, too."

"Long time ago. How's your family?"

"Fine. The kids are healthy, and Pete's business is thriving."

"Pete's a lucky guy."

"He knows it," she said, with the same delightful, lilting laugh that I sometimes heard in my quiet moments.

She swiveled toward the window and crossed her still shapely legs.

"It was something to do with a bungled Ponzi scheme, wasn't it?"

She was talking about Sully, trying to recall the allegations that triggered his downfall.

"Something like that," I said. "Some money kind of went missing."

"I was just a young assistant then, but as I recall, it was a lot of money."

"It was a lot to me," I said.

"And not much of it ever came back."

"The bar's Client Recovery Fund covered it, so Sully's client was happy."

"George Duggan," she said.

"Is he still around?"

I knew that he was, but I wanted her reaction. She didn't provide one.

"I think he ended up with most of the money."

"He was a smart man," I said.

Heather swiveled back in her chair and smiled at me. Her wistful tone changed along with the subject.

"You were smart, too, Joth. Once Sully turned in his ticket, the bar dropped the entire investigation. Duggan stopped cooperating, and the evidence was never developed. That's what kept Sully out of jail, you know. Is he still blaming you for advising him to accept disbarment?"

"No good deed goes unpunished."

"But that's why we never had enough to indict him. You fixed it. You know that. That's what you do."

"Seemed like a pretty good deal at the time," I said.

"Still does to me," she said. "What's Sully doing for work?"

"You've always had a nice way of sliding into the investigative questions."

"And you've always been very perceptive. I'm glad to see you haven't lost your touch. So what are you here for?"

"Can't this be just a social visit, Heather?"

"It could. But it isn't."

"Okay. Your office, your rules. There's been some tension between Sully and his brother-in-law over Holly's estate."

"Nothing new there. Happens all the time."

"Yeah," I said. "You remember Paul Saunders?"

Heather squinted as she called up the name from her memory bank.

"College friend of yours? Big guy? Bullet head?"

I laughed.

"That's right. Holly was Paul's sister."

She reached again for the paperweight.

"Some problem between Paul and Sully?"

"Yeah, a little bit. As I understand it, Paul is named as his sister's executor under the will. He hasn't qualified yet, but you might say he's already jumped into the job with a fair amount of let's just say, enthusiasm."

I watched Heather closely as I said this, looking for tells: the barely perceptible stiffening of her posture, the tongue darting briefly to her lips. She was a woman of exquisite self-control and even to me, who had seen every emotion on her face, the reaction barely registered, but it was there.

"That happens," she said.

"Yeah, well, Paul claims that there's a laptop missing, and that Sully may have taken it."

Her eyes met mine, and they didn't waver.

"And?"

"Personally, I don't think she ever had a laptop, but if she did, it was still in the house when she died. I'd like to clear up this problem between them if I can."

The moment of self-revelation passed. Heather chuckled and pushed back from her desk.

"So this is just a ploy to get a look at the police inventory?"

"I assume the police took one when they secured the scene?"

"I'm sure they did."

"So, if it's convenient . . ."

She leaned forward and pushed a button on her telephone console.

"Betty, can I have a copy of the inventory for Holly Sullivan? And let's have a copy of the coroner's report, too."

Heather sat back in her chair and looked at me without smiling—all business.

"What else does Paul think?"

"It's not always easy to tell what Paul thinks."

"On the contrary," she said. "From the little I recall, he was always as transparent as glass."

"I've never had your gift for personal insight."

"No, you haven't," she said through a sigh.

Betty knocked on the door and entered. She placed a slim file folder on the center of Heather's desk and left without a word to either of us.

"That was quick," I said.

Heather ran a tight ship, but Betty couldn't have found the file so quickly unless she was working on it.

Heather opened the folder and leafed through it, studying each of the few documents it contained. She pulled one out, turned it over, made sure the back was blank and handed it across to me. It was the inventory, and I scanned it quickly. There was no mention at all of a laptop.

"A lot of Diazepam."

"And none of it in containers marked that way," Heather said. "Where do you suppose she got it?"

"She could have gotten it anywhere. She had friends in low places. You know that."

"Sure."

Heather shifted her posture, and I guessed she was weighing her words.

"So let me see if I have this straight, Joth. Your client's wife is dead, and you want to know if my office is investigating her death?"

"I know you are, Heather. Unattended deaths are always investigated in this Commonwealth."

She studied another document from the file before pushing it across her desk to me. It was a preliminary death certificate. My eyes scanned down the page to Cause of Death. In the blank, someone had typed: "Overdose of Diazepam."

"Can I take a copy of this?"

"No," she said.

I could hear the peevishness in her voice. I was pushing too hard.

"Okay, but it seems like there's a word missing."

"What's that?"

"Accidental."

"Maybe no one's reached that conclusion yet."

"Is that true?"

"It's a little early, Joth, don't you think?"

"I suppose so."

Heather looked at me and waited until I met her eyes.

"You think she was possibly murdered?" she said.

"No, I don't."

"Okay. But let's assume it wasn't an accident."

"All right."

I wanted her views and was willing to let her hear some of mine to get them.

"Who else might have done it?" she said.

"You mean putting aside the possibility of suicide? I can give you four or five alternate theories."

"Really?"

"Yes. She could have gotten Valium from any number of people. It was almost certainly an accident, but even if it wasn't, there are a half-dozen people who had more motive than Sully to kill her."

Heather weighed my words and nodded judiciously.

"Look, as far as we know, she died of an accidental drug overdose and that's how it will stay, absent any new evidence."

I moved on to complete my prior thought.

"But Paul is motivated to provide new or different evidence, and I don't think he's too scrupulous about where it comes from."

"Really?"

"Yes, Heather, really."

"You think Paul Saunders is capable of obstruction of justice?"

I hadn't thought of it that way, but the idea made me laugh.

"That's for you to figure out."

"Joth, you've known me for a long time. I'm not going to bring charges against anyone until I've worked through every possibility."

"That'll take some time."

"It probably will."

"I just don't want Sully sitting in jail while you work it through."

She scratched the inside of her ear.

"Isn't this the part where you promise me he won't be going anyplace?"

"There's no reason for you to even suggest that."

"Have you two discussed it?"

Her question struck a nerve.

"Heather, I'm not telling you what my client and I discussed. You know that."

"All right. Then there's nothing else to talk about, is there?"

I dawdled. I knew that Heather knew more than she was telling me, and I sensed that she had been on the verge of revealing some of it just moments ago.

"I'll be looking into it," she said.

She got up and walked toward the door and I followed her.

"I'd be disappointed in you if you didn't."

I went downstairs and cornered the prosecutor who had my shoplifting case.

Jane Fitzgerald was an overworked and often frazzled assistant who had been in Heather's office for three or four years, long enough to be jaded with the routine.

I showed her the conviction. Jane's conventionally pretty face was marred by a permanent furrow between her bright blues eyes, caused by either nearsightedness or the perpetual sneer of what I could only call disgust.

"What are you going to do with that?" she said.

Her bark was sharp, as if she didn't know.

I waved it at her.

"Your witness was the guy found with the binoculars, if you recall. The only reason he isn't the defendant is because he got to the police first and rolled over on my guy."

"Lazy police work. So what? Your guy's still guilty."

"Is he? You think the judge is going to convict my guy based on the testimony of a witness holding hot merchandise with a recent fraud conviction?"

"Go ahead and try it," she said.

I looked around at a hallway teeming with hungry defense lawyers, bored witnesses, and anxious defendants.

"You try all these cases, Jane, you'll be here 'til midnight. You can get this one off your docket right now."

She followed my eyes.

"Okay, Joth. He pleads guilty to trespassing. Fifty dollar fine, and he stays out of the store for a year."

"Done."

Twenty minutes later, I was back in my office. The coffee was stale from yesterday, but I drank it anyway.

Chapter Six

A Night at the Caps

Most of the friends I shared with Sully were college buddies of mine who gravitated to northern Virginia after graduation. Kevin Riley, who texted me the news of Holly's death, was one of the few friends I'd met through Sully.

Like Sully, he was a native of Skaneateles, New York, a small town near Syracuse. It was pure coincidence that the two childhood friends ended up in northern Virginia, where Riley's mother's family had extensive commercial and residential real estate holdings. After earning his business degree from one of the SUNY schools, Riley relocated to North Arlington and took on the management of Riley Properties. It was natural that he became Sully's client and bringing his business to the Regan firm was part of what marked Sully as a rising star in the firm's real estate practice.

For a fair amount of time, Sully's ethical debacle tied up several of Riley's properties, an inconvenience he weathered with more patience and grace than I could have mustered. They had too much history between them for that to chill their friendship for long, in part because Riley was a man of tremendous personal loyalty.

They were so close that Riley appeared at the foreclosure sale of Sully's house. When the hammer went down on the sale, Riley put his arm around Sully's shoulder and offered him decent housing at a reduced rental. Sully was willing to sign a lease, but Riley magnanimously rejected the offer with a wave of his hand, a gesture he would live to regret.

I called him at his office at two in the afternoon. Other than our exchange about Holly's death, we hadn't spoken in a year or two. After a few minutes of small talk, I got to the point.

"I've got two tickets to the Caps game tonight. Interested?

"Sure. Who they playing?"

"Buffalo."

"Even better. I hate those bastards."

"Cheer for anybody you want, but I suggest you wear a red shirt as a matter of self-preservation."

I heard him chuckle.

"I'll pick you up at 6:30. You still live in the same place?"

"Haven't moved in years, Joth."

Riley lived so close to McLean that the Arlington-Fairfax County line ran through his backyard. He'd built here when this local address meant real money on both the tax rolls and in the real estate market, but he never intended to sell. Good thing, too, because the faux Tudor monstrosity of his had not aged well.

Nor had his wife, for that matter. Mandy Riley had never been part of the gang, and her lukewarm reception told me that her distrust toward those who had shared her husband's wild years had not faded with time. She invited me in, but Riley was already pulling a denim jacket over the kind of red sweatshirt that had become *de rigeur* at Washington Capitals home games.

Riley was conventionally handsome with a mop of graying hair and a quick, wide smile. He stood an inch or two taller than my six feet one and so painfully thin that he called to mind a cyclist or a tennis player. He had never played a sport as far as I knew, but he followed all of the Washington teams with an unusual passion and intensity.

"How'd you get the tickets?" he said, as he slipped into the passenger seat of my aging Volvo.

"Client."

"He didn't pay you, right?"

"He says he will."

Riley shrugged at what he perceived to be my naïveté.

"Once you accept the tickets, that's the kiss of death."

He was also a shrewd businessman.

"Maybe, but I've got a feeling this guy's going to need me again."

He chuckled.

"Don't forget to charge interest," he said.

Our conversation turned to the Caps, and he knew much more about them than I did.

Ovechkin-mania was in full swing in Washington that spring. Led by Russian man-child Alex Ovechkin, the Caps had developed a hard-charging offensive style that accomplished two things that rarely happened in the Caps' history: winning games and filling seats. The Arena was awash in red as we took our seats just below the concourse at the upper edge of the lower bowl. Riley bought two beers on the way in and promised two more at the second intermission.

As an attentive sports fan, Riley seemed to seek out and draw conclusions from the telling details that separate winners from losers in every athletic endeavor, from the Masters to the Tour de France. He noted wingers skating with fresh legs, defensemen appearing distracted, and centers who shied away from physical contact. For most of the first period he sat with his chin in his hand, fingertips on his lips as he absorbed the flow of play. His observations were few, but always incisive. He concluded that it was the Caps' night before either team had scored a goal.

With the Caps up 3 to 1 and the clock dwindling down to end the second period, Riley remembered his promise of a second round of beers and excused himself to beat the intermission rush. When he returned, most of the patrons were still out on the concourse and the Zamboni occupied the ice. He sat down and took a long drink of beer.

"Hockey and Molsen beer," he said, lifting his plastic cup in a toast. "Canada's only useful exports."

I raised mine.

"And Neil Young."

"And Joni Mitchell," he said. "And natural energy if this country would be smart enough to tap the Canadian oil reserves."

I was one of the few residents of the metropolitan D.C. area without political convictions and had become adept at ducking that type of loaded conversation, but this night was different.

"And generic drugs," I said.

"You're right!" he said, brightening. "People like me would save a hell of a lot of money if the FDA would approve what they make in Canada. It's the insurance companies, you know, and every congressman and senator has their hand out for a check from as many of them as they can manage."

"And you're going to need a lot more of those medications as you get older."

"Damn right," Riley said. "And don't think Medicare's going to pay for them."

"They're costing me too much now."

"Tell me about it!" he said. "I'm on two blood pressure medications, and my wife takes more medications than I can count. Probably why my blood pressure's so high."

"Is that anything to worry about?"

"Not really. She takes something for asthma and something for lupus."

"That's a tough story."

"Enough to drive me to drink. She also takes a sedative, and now you know why."

"A sedative?" I said. "I'm not surprised. Everyone seems to be taking something these days."

"Yeah, in her case it's Valium, and that adds up. And don't forget I'm self-insured."

Riley's rage against the government continued for a few minutes and subsided when the second period began. I let it go. I'd heard what I'd come to hear. Even Kevin Riley, as upstanding a citizen as any in Arlington

County, Virginia, had the means to have killed Holly Sullivan.

Sully would occupy his real estate without paying until he had someplace else to go. That was a flimsy motive, but people have killed for less, and Heather knew it.

No matter what she might think Sully had done, she wouldn't indict him if I could point the finger at others with a motive and opportunity, or who might otherwise benefit from her death. The more reasonable doubt I could develop, the less likely it was that she could get a conviction and that was how the game was played.

As the Caps' one-sided victory wound down, the roar of the crowd became deafening. Riley leaned toward me to speak.

"I don't suppose this is purely social; you inviting me to a hockey game so soon after Holly's death?"

I wondered for a moment if he connected our discussion about Valium, but that could be easily denied.

"This is just a couple of old friends getting together, Riley."

"Okay," he said through a disbelieving sigh.

The false pretenses bothered me. As the final siren sounded and the crowd began to file out, I decided to quiz Riley a little further.

"All right. I'm curious."

"About what?"

"You ever do any business with Paul Saunders?"

"A little. Not much. He tried to jump in with me when Sully went down. To tell you the truth, I don't like the guy much. And I certainly don't trust him."

As I sat for a minute, staring at the ice, Riley filled the silence.

"Did Sully hire you?"

"Let's just say he wants me to monitor a very fluid situation."

"Then you can ask him when he's going to get out of my house and pay me the back rent."

"You can ask him yourself. There he is."

A hockey fan from the cradle, Sully had been on the leading edge of the "Rock the Red" wave and despite everything that had happened to him, he remained a season ticket holder. He was directly below us, four rows behind the Capitals bench, standing with his slim, lovely—and much younger—girlfriend, along with the rest of the diehards applauding the victorious Caps.

"That son of a bitch," said Riley. "What's he doing here?"

"He's at every home game."

Riley flopped back in his seat, his arms folded across his chest.

"So he can't pay my rent, but he can pay for Caps tickets?"

I sipped my beer.

"I wonder if Dan Crowley knows about this."

"Dan Crowley?" I said.

"Sully owes Dan more than he owes me."

"Are we talking about Irish Dan Crowley? Down in Crystal City?"

"That's the guy," said Riley.

"He owns a strip bar."

I knew that because I occasionally defended his girls, some of whom seemed to collect misdemeanor charges––and sometimes felonies—like folded, one-dollar bills.

Riley acted like he was offended on his friend's behalf.

"Dan's got his hands in a lot of stuff. For one thing, he buys up notes and other obligations at a discount and then collects on them."

I was unaware of this.

"He's factoring?"

"Factoring."

Riley pronounced the word as if he was sampling it.

"No, I wouldn't say he's factoring, Joth. That implies some sort of a system. If you know Dan, and I bet you do, you know he's the kind of guy who sees an oppor- tunity and just sort of jumps in."

I nodded slightly, not wanting to let Riley know how much I knew about Dan.

"How can Dan collect a debt that the creditor can't?" I said. "Dan's a pussy cat."

"Because Dan is friends with Jimmie Flambeau," he said.

"Sully owes Dan money?"

"Joth, Sully owes a lot of people money. Maybe I should sell my debt to Irish Dan. Or Jimmie Flambeau."

I knew he wouldn't. Jimmie Flambeau was a scary guy, and no matter how much Sully owed him, Riley wouldn't put his old friend on the spot. He was a bigger pussy cat than Irish Dan. No matter how hard Riley raged, threatened or cajoled, Sully would be his unpaying tenant until *he* decided to move out.

Chapter Seven

Nine Ball

The Commonwealth Attorney's office always offers plea deals on the morning of a trial. Confident in the knowledge that they secure convictions in 90 percent of their cases, one of their lawyers will float something just a little better than a convicting judge or jury would probably hand down. Then the bargaining begins. You can trade community service time for an increase in the amount of the fine, or maybe accept a conviction for a lesser offense, structuring a deal around your client's tolerance for different sorts of judicially imposed pain.

I've always resented the process. You reject a plea at your client's discretion, but also at their risk. Usually they ask, "What would you do?" and I usually answer, "It doesn't matter what I'd do." But it does to them, because I am the one with the knowledge and experience and my judgment is part of what they are paying me to use.

As a younger man, I played this game with more enthusiasm and commitment, working with my clients to assure an individualized deal and a result they could abide. More recently, I'd become aware that the process was corrupting me, leaving me jaded and disgusted at the assembly line quality of justice in our local court system. This had reduced me to another faceless cog in the machinery. It was a process, I knew, that began with my representation of Sully in the George Duggan matter.

On a beautiful, early spring day, after convincing a young prosecutor to reduce a DWI to a charge of reckless driving and to waive the suspension of my client's license, I shook every extended hand as I exited the courthouse. I walked down Wilson Boulevard to Whitlow's, where I often had lunch at the bar.

Whitlow's was an old-line Arlington establishment; one of the last remaining outposts of the familiar, friendly and slightly seedy Clarendon section of the county. It had thrived in the years before development dollars turned Clarendon into a destination for the young professionals now occupying and renovating what used to be the modest and sleepy neighborhoods of North Arlington.

It was early and Whitlow's was quiet. Johnny was behind the bar, dressed in an open-necked white shirt and apron. He brought me an iced coffee without being asked.

"Friend of yours back there," he said, jerking his head toward a narrow pool room off the bar.

Back in our younger, better days, Sully and I would sometimes while away a winter afternoon there, shooting nine-ball, watching hockey and swapping five-dollar bills over small wagers. Johnny was about my age and we had shared a lot of the same ups and downs. I looked at him and he nodded through a sour expression.

The pool room was two steps down through a narrow doorway. I saw one person in there: Sully, working through a layout on an eight-foot table of chewed-up green felt. He was leaning over a shot, but he looked up when my shadow fell across the table.

"Joth Proctor," he said. "Trolling for clients?"

"I'll bet you a beer you miss that shot."

He saluted me with a half-empty mug and drained it. Then he drained the shot, a difficult combination, as well.

"Heineken?"

Sully grinned and I walked back to the bar where I held up two fingers for Johnny.

"Looks like he's putting 'em down pretty quick to-day," Johnny said.

He filled two mugs from the tap.

"This'll be his fourth."

"He can still handle it," I said.

Johnny caught my eye as he slid the mugs across to me.

"Not like he used to."

"I guess I'd better go see if his pool game has improved."

"I doubt it," Johnny said, with a grunt.

I wondered if Sully was also in hock to Whitlow's.

Sully had grown up around pool tables, and from the day I met him, he had all the makings of a superb nine-ball player. He was a tremendous strategist with the ability to see his way through a rack from the break. He was also a great shot maker with the steady nerves of the gambler he purported to be. After losing his license, he tried his hand on the pro tour for a time. He qualified for several tournaments and did all right, but he never won enough money to make a living, at least not the kind he was used to making.

A rack of warped, single-piece bar cues was fixed to one wood-paneled wall. Beside them on a shelf sat Sully's cue case. Back in the good days, Sully had a nine-foot championship table in a room above his garage. The competition cue and carrying case was one of the few things that had survived the foreclosure.

I put the second mug on the shelf next to the carrying case. Sully hefted it and took a long drink.

"What a surprise," I said, "seeing you here, Sully."

"Joth, if I wanted to see you, I'd go to your office. Grab a cue."

I picked a stick arbitrarily, not bothering to measure its condition and began to chalk it up. He racked the balls.

"Dollar a game?"

I nodded. It was worth that to watch him play.

"You break."

He bent over and immediately pocketed a ball.

What Sully lacked wasn't skill, it was the discipline to practice daily, especially once he lost the big house with its elegant tournament table. But more critically, he lacked the discipline to eschew the showy, low-percentage shot for the smart play; for the safe, conservative shot that would keep his opponent on defense.

When he missed a bank shot on the four, probably on purpose, I took a moment to consider my options.

"Maybe it's time for you and me to go on the road," he said.

It was an old joke and I acknowledged it with a chuckle, but I couldn't help wondering what he'd say if I agreed. I made the four and missed the five, and he wasted no time cleaning up after me.

"Another?" he said.

"Sure."

Sully was a grifter at heart. Part of him would like nothing better than to live out of a suitcase, traveling from town to town and motel room to motel room, hustling strangers for dinner money. He'd love it for about a week, and then wonder how I'd ever talked him into it.

"So what are you doing down here on a Tuesday afternoon?"

"Bored," he said.

I believed him. But I also knew he figured I might be here. He stopped by because he wanted to talk.

"I saw Heather," I said.

"How's she looking?"

"Pretty good for a woman her age."

"You mean our age."

I racked the balls and sat on a barstool. He nodded and pursed his lips. I appreciated him letting it go. Dry break. He swore and sat down.

"What did she want?" he said.

I got up and sunk the first three, then missed an easy bank shot.

"A lot of things. She wanted to know where you were when your wife died."

"Fine," said Sully. "All she has to do is tell me when she died."

I looked at him and waited.

"She was alive the last time I saw her," he said. "I told you that."

"Yeah, but I had to drag it out of you, Sully."

"Does Heather think I killed her?"

"I don't think she's a woman who jumps to conclusions," I said.

Sully finished his beer and chuckled again before returning to a question I had asked him in the parking lot of my office.

"Let me ask it differently. Do you think Holly was murdered?"

The lack of emotion in his voice as he spoke about his wife chilled me.

"Sully, you have to start by asking who had a motive to kill her. That list starts with you."

"Me and about a dozen others, Joth. But I don't think anyone had the will to kill her, and that's something different."

"That's a fair point."

"And it's something someone has to explain to Heather."

Sully leaned out the door, yelled Johnny's name and ordered another round.

"Name me someone else with a motive," I said.

"Sure. That son of a bitch who dates my daughter, for one."

"Barry. You mentioned his name."

"Did I? Well, he plays lacrosse with Dave. Not a friend of his, an acquaintance really. I don't think Dave likes him anymore than I do. The kid's a real pig."

As far as I knew, Sully's son, Dave, had always been an up-standing kid. I didn't peg him as someone with dangerous friends, so I was skeptical of where Sully might be steering this speculation.

"That doesn't mean he killed anybody," I said.

Johnny came in with two beers and placed them on the shelf next to the cues. Sully threw a ten on Johnny's tray without acknowledging him, picked up his mug, and took a long drink, waiting for Johnny to leave.

"Okay, Joth, what do you think about this? Dave's on a travel team with Barry last fall. They win the title and this pig decides to celebrate by making some marijuana brownies. Somehow, Holly gets wind of it and tips off the school authorities."

"She must have really hated Barry," I said.

"Holly was a lot of things, but smart wasn't one of 'em. She figured it wouldn't go beyond the school, and anyway, they were all minors, so, you know, it was a tough-love sort of thing. Turns out it was on school property, but school's not in session. Plus, Barry just turned eighteen. He gets arrested for possession. Holly thought since they were all still underage, they'd get a slap on the wrist and it would get expunged when he turned eighteen. Typical Holly. She fucked that up and the kid's got a record."

"That's a terrible story."

"It is for Barry," said Sully. "And for Sarah, too."

"Anybody else implicated?"

"Not as far as I know. Not Dave, anyway. Holly was right about one thing: they let the minors off. Dave was barely seventeen at the time."

"351 disposition for Barry?"

Yeah," Sully shrugged. "First offender status, so the punk didn't get a conviction, but he's still got an arrest record. And he lost his lacrosse scholarship."

"And you think that's enough for him to kill your wife?"

He thoughtfully slugged down a mouthful of beer.

"Of course not. I'm just saying."

"What *are* you saying?"

"I'm saying Barry's a lax bro. He thinks the world's his oyster, and the normal rules don't apply to him."

"Sounds like somebody else I know," I said, making sure Sully caught my eye.

I had been a lacrosse player, too, but Sully embodied all the offensive stereotypes. He glared at me for a moment and then let the whole thing go. I returned to the original question.

"Who else might have killed her?"

"Duggan."

"George Duggan, your former—?"

"I said maybe."

"Why would he want to kill her?" I said.

"A debt."

Sully said this bitterly, without looking at me.

"She owed him money?"

"I didn't say she owed him money, but she owed him."

I bent over an easy shot and missed it.

"So did you, Sully."

"We're talking about Holly."

He quickly lined up a shot and struck it violently, dropping the five ball in the corner pocket.

"He put her where she is today."

Sully paused and corrected himself.

"I mean, where she spent the last six years of her life."

As I listened to his tone, I felt the repressed hatred Sully still harbored for the man who ruined him.

"And?"

"She had a lot of dirt on him," said Sully.

"Where'd she get that from?"

"I might have told her."

"Come on, Sully. She was blackmailing him?"

"Might have been."

"With what?"

"She knows where all the bodies were buried," he said.

That sure sounded vague.

"Duggan's a dangerous guy to fool with," I said.

"No kidding."

Sully stepped back to line up a shot.

"Or maybe she was blackmailing Jimmie Flambeau?" he said.

"Jimmie Flambeau?" I said.

"Maybe I've had too much to drink, Joth. Point is, if Heather's making a list of people with a grudge against Holly, it's a pretty long list, and my name sure as hell shouldn't be first."

"As of now, Sully, the only one making a list is Paul, and yours is the only name on it."

"Paul?"

He scowled and swore pungently.

"You know the only thing Paul wants?"

"Yeah," I said. "He wants the property."

Sully backed away from the shot and looked at me with surprise.

"You talk to him?"

"Yeah, I did."

I changed the facts a little, hoping to generate a response.

"He said you two had some deal to develop it."

"There was some talk about developing it, yeah, but it was just talk. There was never any deal."

I nodded. I knew how a guy like Paul would picture it.

"Paul would do the work and you'd share in the profits," I said. "Is that how it was supposed to work?"

Sully leaned over and made the seven without even looking.

"Something like that, Joth. But it was just talk."

"Then you inherit the property and you cut him out."

"Why not? It's my house," he said.

I waited, leaning on my cue. Sully eyed the eight ball. It was a simple, straight-on shot, but he missed it.

"He was trying to push me out," he said. "Anyway, he hasn't got the juice to develop a property like that."

"So you cut him out?"

"Like I said, the deal was just talk; never more than that."

"But now you own it," I said.

"Yeah. Now I own it. It's your fuckin' shot."

I missed; he ran the table, and I racked the balls. We started another game in tense silence. Then Sully said:

"You coming to the wake?" Sully said out of nowhere. "Tomorrow night at O'Brien's."

"First I've heard of it. You're not going to get much of a crowd if you don't get the word out."

"Word's out, Joth. Don't worry."

"I never worry about anything you plan, Sully," I said. "Maybe I should."

He laughed.

I chalked up the cue and waited for my next shot.

Chapter Eight

Irish Dan

The Riding Time gentlemen's club, with no windows, minimal signage and even less parking, was tucked away in Crystal City in a narrow space between a 7-11 and a Chinese restaurant. Once inside, the pulsing back beat of the jukebox hit me like a wave of stifling body heat and the cigar smoke idled up against a low ceiling. A bar occupied the far end of the space and in the center, a number of small tables turned to face a semi-circular stage set, against the wall. A slender, curvy girl decked out in a G-string and pasties was working the pole onstage. I sat down at a table where I could see the bar.

At three o'clock on a weekday afternoon, Congress was in session, which meant a key clientele had not yet filled the joint. Even the government workers who habitually took long lunch hours there were elsewhere by then.

Before long, Dan Crowley appeared behind the bar. He was big and balding, with clear blue eyes in a welcoming face. His convivial, unshakeable friendliness was a key to his success, but he was a shrewd business-man. Buying and selling unsecured loans required the agile mind of an accountant and the cajones of a matador, and Irish Dan looked like he had neither. I noticed the tail of his button-down shirt was half untucked, as if he'd just emerged hurriedly from the john.

That's when I caught his eye and stepped over to greet him.

"Joth Proctor! Look what the cat dragged in." he said.

He gave me a firm, full-bodied hug. Dan had a pretty good case of body odor, as anyone would have who spent more than an hour in that hotbox. I waited for him to sit down and followed suit.

"Just seeing if any of your girls might need some legal assistance."

Dan laughed as if we had just shared an inside joke.

"Or me, maybe?"

"Or you, Dan. You never know in this town."

I'd represented one of his dancers in the only case I'd ever handled that had gained notoriety. A member of the Virginia General Assembly had been found dead in a Crystal City motel. One of Dan's girls had been with him. When the investigating police found a vial of cocaine on the nightstand, Jewel was arrested and immediately charged with possession, possession with intent to distribute, and manslaughter.

Jewel was smart enough to keep her mouth shut until Dan called me to the scene. In the end, they couldn't prove ownership of the cocaine, and medical tests showed that the state delegate had died of a heart attack, brought on by the exertions of the evening, unaided by any foreign substance.

"Not the worst way to go," Dan had noted at the time.

Amen to that.

"Jewel still working for you?"

"No," he said. "She moved to the West Coast. Gonna get into movies. I think she'll be great."

"Yeah," I said.

I could only imagine.

"So how's business, Dan?"

He ignored the question. Small talk was over.

"Joth, what are you really doing here?"

"Working for Tom Sullivan."

"I see, hmm."

He settled back in the chair and looked at me like he was thinking about an investment I had just pitched. The smile never left his puffy lips, but he studied my face like a doctor looking for signs that his medicine was working.

"I heard his wife died."

"Ex-wife."

"I knew that."

"Do you know what she died of?"

"I heard it was a heart attack," he said, shaking his head somberly. "Awful young for a heart attack, huh?"

I assumed Dan knew the truth.

"Apparently, there were some people who didn't like her," I said.

"No, I don't think so."

This was a man who didn't want any trouble from anybody.

"You don't miss much, do you, Dan?"

"I try not to, Joth; I try not to. Sully got any other loose ends to tie up?"

"Yeah, you might say so."

The dancer on the stage stepped down, her set at an end. She pulled on a lime-green negligee and made a beeline for my table.

"I'm Jade," she said.

Irish Dan gave them nicknames and I could see where hers came from. She had startlingly green eyes and copper colored hair that set them off to further advantage. I took out a ten and handed it to her, thanking her for a performance I hadn't watched. She gave me a wink that was more amiable than lascivious.

Too old for her, I reflected. Dan pursed his lips and nodded approvingly.

"What's Sully worried about?"

I turned my palms up, indicating a slight shrug.

"As you say, loose ends. For one thing, I understand there's an issue of debt."

Dan looked at his fingernails.

"Sully doesn't owe me money. Maybe his wife did. But you tell Sully that with me, people's debts die with them. They don't pass on and they don't get inherited."

Another girl was already up on the pole. I glanced at her as I processed Irish Dan's response.

"That's generous of you."

"It's not generous," he said. "It's just good business."

"How did Holly work up those kind of debts?"

"Gambling," said Dan. "That's what I hear. College football, if you can believe it."

"Jimmie Flambeau?" I said.

Dan nodded.

"That's usually the guy."

"So she probably owed somebody else more money than she owed you."

"I would say that's a good bet."

"I'm sure you're right, Dan."

"Anything else I can do for you?" he said.

I stood up and took a deep breath.

"Yeah, what do you know about George Duggan?"

Dan slowly rose to his feet.

"I know he was tangled up with your friend."

"That was years ago. How 'bout now?"

"I understand he's got a big real-estate deal going in North Arlington."

"Would it surprise you if somebody was blackmailing him?" I said.

Irish Dan smiled, appreciating the question.

"It would surprise me if someone wasn't."

I nodded.

"How 'bout Jimmie Flambeau?"

Dan stared at me and didn't say a word. That was too big of a question to ask and we both knew it.

"Remind Sully that he's still alive, and he needs to fully live," he said, and winked. "Would you do that for me, Joth?"

"There's a wake tomorrow night."

"No, you just tell him," Dan said.

He smiled, as if he'd asked me to impart happy birthday wishes.

"Sure, Dan. And let me know next time one of your girls gets into trouble."

"You know I will, Joth. I surely will."

I shook his hand and left.

***

I knew my way around the courthouse well enough that by the next morning I had already gathered the basics of what the Arlington's defense bar now referred to as the Brownie Bust. Sully's outline was generally accurate. Court records for minors are sealed, but two of the kids swept up in the process had been over eighteen. Their records provided an outline I could fill in, based on experience and a chat with the arresting officer, Chris Kelleher, who worked security at Yorktown High School.

In Arlington, each of the three public high schools is assigned a full-time police officer, whose job it is to defuse any little squabbles that can become big problems and to handle the ones that are big to begin with. Tact and discretion in dealing with kids of a delicate age— and their hard-charging, ambitious parents—is paramount, so it shouldn't have surprised me that Chris Kelleher was a woman.

I found her that afternoon at the high school, patrolling the walkway between the lacrosse stadium and the girls' softball diamond. I thought it ludicrous that she wore a bulletproof vest and more gadgets around her hips than Batman, but the paramilitary regalia couldn't hide her voluptuous curves. I was confident that Sully must have had the same first impression.

The softball diamond was below street level and the adjacent lacrosse stadium. The stone wall of the walkway that separated the two fields formed the top section of the left field wall of the softball field. Kelleher was leaning on the wall with her hands folded placidly before her as she watched a spirited softball game against a district rival unfolding on the field below. She had piercing blue eyes and a sun-hardened complexion that would soon make her prematurely old, but she looked just fine for someone I guessed was in her early-forties.

I walked up to her and introduced myself as Tom Sullivan's lawyer. She regarded me with a twinkle of amusement that I rarely saw in a police officer's eyes.

"Now what's Mr. Sullivan need a lawyer for this time?"

"He's worried about repercussions from the events of last fall."

"Really?"

"The Brownie Bust."

"I would think that's a civil matter at this point."

"That may be, but how that plays out could depend on what you can tell me."

Kelleher turned back to the field, resumed her casual posture, and shook her head.

"I can't tell you anything I haven't already told Tom."

"Tom? Nobody calls him by his given name."

That knocked her down a peg.

"Mr. Sullivan, excuse me."

I nodded and looked at her as if I'd missed something.

"Yeah, well Sully doesn't always get the facts quite right," I said.

My attention was drawn to the crack of a bat.

"Nice play by the third baseman," she said.

I leaned up beside her, as if engrossed in the game. She seemed to consider my last comment and laughed, a pleasant, high-pitched sound; something I would have expected from one of the teenage softball players below us.

"No, he doesn't always do that; does he?" she said.

"He's a little worried about this kid Barry," I said, "you know; what he might do and what he might have already done."

"I assure you he's been given several stern lectures and there will be no further repercussions," she said.

"I was that age once," I said. "Believe me, that only goes so far."

She smirked at me.

"Yes, but he's a smart kid."

"Sully doesn't like him because he's screwing his daughter," I said, "if you don't mind a little frankness."

She didn't seem to.

"He knows Dave did what any good team captain would have done. Plus, Dave's about twice the kid's size. He's not gonna go looking for any revenge."

"Dave?" I said. "I heard Holly blew the whistle."

"She did. But Dave didn't want his mom in the middle of that, so he took the hit for it. He's a stand-up kid."

I turned away and watched the softball game for a few minutes.

"These kids are pretty good," I said.

"So's the lacrosse team. Look, boys are different than girls, although I shouldn't have to tell that to a man of your age. That happens to a girl. She'll hold a grudge forever unless she can steal the other girl's prom date. Boys? They take a couple of swings at each other and it's over."

"Is that what Barry did when he heard that Dave turned him in?" I said.

"You'll have to ask the participants," she said, a typical police response.

"But it cost him his scholarship," I said.

"It cost him his scholarship, but he's still going to college. His family has money. Besides, what's he gonna sue Dave for?"

"Four years' of lost tuition?" I said.

She considered my idea before answering.

"Those are the only damages," she said, "and it's probably his parents' claim, anyway, right? 'Course, I'm not a lawyer, but no, I don't think there's any cause of action against Dave. He was only reporting a crime. Besides, as you say, Barry was screwing Dave's sister."

She glanced at me a second, as if to see how I would respond.

"You have kids?" she said.

"No, I'm not married. You?"

"I've got two boys in middle school," she said, shaking her head. "I'm not looking forward to the next six years."

"And your husband shares your views?"

"Ex-husband. If he did, we'd probably still be married."

"Yeah, well, thanks for your time," I said.

"It wasn't much," she said, in a tone I thought sounded hopeful.

"You never know," I said, trying not to smile as I left.

As I walked away, I thought she'd be perfect for Sully.

Chapter Nine

Holly's Farewell

I had to hand it to Sully. He threw a hell of a going away party for a woman he no longer called his wife. He even went to the trouble of locating a small funeral parlor near Fort Myer, run by a pair of Irish brothers who didn't object to the copious amounts of food and liquor he proposed to make available.

He arranged for two rooms—one with the open casket and prayer railing, and an adjacent room that sucked in the guests like a roulette wheel in a casino. It contained a table covered in fruit, vegetables and cold cuts, and another with a full bar and a bartender dressed in a white dinner jacket, mixing drinks like someone just got married. People flowed from one to the other, but I didn't notice anyone paying much attention to Holly.

The open coffin shocked me. I'd known Holly since her brother Paul was an eager-to-please, walk-on midfielder and she was a sassy prom queen, ready to play with the big boys in Charlottesville.

Nobody looks good in a coffin, but she looked like hell—emaciated and aged far beyond her years.

Wondering what perverse impulse had caused Sully to agree to an open casket, I knelt before it and stumbled through a few Hail Marys, reflecting on the hard ride that life had given this old friend.

The amount of people who had gathered to pay their final respects surprised me almost as much as Holly's appearance. There were lawyers, politicians, real-estate developers and local businessmen. There were friends of the kids, friends of the family, and friends of friends, looking for a free sandwich or a nice, stiff drink.

This is what happens when you die young, I thought. People come out of the woodwork.

I bumped into one of them as I stood up: Jimmie Flambeau was a small, neat package of a man. He wore a black suit with an immaculate white silk shirt, a dark tie and a white handkerchief tucked perfectly into the breast pocket. His thick black hair was moussed, and he wore a pair of dark-rimmed glasses with thick lenses.

"Joth Proctor," he said.

He took my hand before I could recall his name.

"Terrible thing, isn't it?"

Jimmie looked grim. But then Jimmie Flambeau always looked grim. He had the demeanor of an undertaker and was said to be the most joyless man in Arlington.

His attendance at the wake put me off.

"I didn't know you knew her, Jimmie."

"We were members of the same church."

"I see," I said, swallowing that scary image. I didn't ask what church.

"Did you know her well, Joth?"

I turned and glanced at the coffin.

"Yeah, I did."

He looked at me inquisitively.

"You're a Massachusetts boy, aren't you Joth?"

"Me? Yes."

"Salem, I think?"

"I went to college with Holly's brother."

"Yes, the UVA boy."

For the first time, a smile appeared on Jimmie's thin, birdlike face.

"If you're ever interested in a little action on the Cavaliers. Or the Wahoos, as you call them . . ."

He let the thought trail off.

So . . . Flambeau knew where I went to college and even where I was born. He carefully cultivated the image of a man with the personal information of strangers at his fingertips. Through these kinds of gestures, and the thugs that usually accompanied him, Jimmie Flambeau presented an unmistakable air of menace. He thought it enhanced his sinister reputation and he was right.

"Thanks Jimmie," I said. "I'll let you know,"

I pushed past him and returned to the other room, where the crowd was so large it spilled out into the hallway. When I got out there, I saw Heather Burke, sipping a drink and wearing a dowdy, A-line dress, as if she expected to blend into the crowd unnoticed.

"What are you doing here?" I said, trying to approach as calmly as I could.

Heather seemed startled by my troubled expression and took a sip of what looked like mineral water. She had her hair pulled back in a bun beneath the kind of scarf Catholic women used to wear to Mass, a style I'd rarely seen on anyone else.

"I've known Sully almost as long as you have. Maybe not as well."

"I hope not."

Her faced opened into a disarming smile.

"I'm just paying my respects. It's a lot of water under the bridge, Joth."

What she said hit me like a glass of cold water. It was sometimes hard for me to see Heather as anything other than the top county prosecutor, or the girl who had dropped me like a hot rock. But now I saw that those youthful days when we were a popular foursome at everything from Bench-and-Bar dinners to Redskins games had resonance for her, too. I wondered if the sight of Sully would rekindle those happy memories of our old friendship. I doubted it, but considering the possibility was unavoidable.

"Have you talked to Sully?" I said.

"No, he's been pretty busy."

"Yeah, I suppose so."

"He could always draw a crowd," said Heather. "Still can."

"Not always for the right reason, though."

"But it was different then," she said wistfully. "Everything was simple then."

"It didn't seem so at the time."

"Youth is wasted on the young, right, Joth? I'll say something to Sully and get out of here."

"Good idea. I think I'll do the same thing."

"Do you have time for a drink?" she said.

Her eyes sparkled for a moment.

"I mean, some place other than here?"

I'm sure I must have stared at her for far too long, probably with my mouth hanging open like the hooked fish I still was.

"No, Heather, I really have to -- get back to the office."

"Sure," she said. "Just a thought."

"Another time."

"Sure," she said.

I watched her disappear into the crowd. She eventually left, but not soon enough.

For the first hour or so, Sully walked around with the self-satisfied expression of a man presiding over his daughter's coming-out party. The next time I saw him, he was steaming. He walked over to me mouthing obscenities and staring past me at Heather, who was deep in conversation with Sully's former brother-in-law.

"She's just paying her respects," I said, trying to cool him down.

"Or performing her civic duty."

"Prosecutors are sometimes off-duty," I said agreeably, "just like anyone else."

"Not her. Not Heather. She's snooping. Look who she's talking to."

"She's known Paul almost as long as she's known you," I said.

Sully wasn't looking at me. He was glaring bitterly over my shoulder at Paul.

"Let it go, Sully."

"You tell her what I told you? That there are lots of people with a motive?"

I remembered what Officer Kelleher had said about Dave's involvement in the Brownie Bust.

"Like Barry?"

"Yeah, like Barry."

"Funny, Sully, because the scuttlebutt I picked up says it was your son who blew the whistle on Barry, not Holly."

"Where'd you get that from?"

"Around the courthouse."

"What were you doing there?"

I let that pass. No point going there.

"As I understand," I said, "Holly had nothing to do with it."

"It's complicated."

"Most things are."

"Don't think so much," Sully said. "You'll get a headache."

I took that under consideration as I worked my way over to Paul. He was drunk as a lord and it was only to preempt his time and keep him from Sully that I backed him into a corner, where I again expressed my condolences.

"You see the coroner's report?" he said. "Came out this morning."

"Where would I have seen that?"

I wondered if he had gotten his information from Heather.

"Accidental death by drug overdose," he said.

"That's what we all expected. I think this should be the end of it."

"Are you representing Sully?"

"Representing him on what?"

Paul looked at me and took a deep breath.

"You think that's the end of it, Joth?"

His voice was rising, which concerned me.

"I just said that it was."

I looked around. Nobody was taking notice of Paul's increased volume.

"I think everybody needs to move on," I said, "if that's what you mean."

"You know who called me today?" said Paul.

I shrugged.

"Guy from the insurance company."

"What insurance company?" I said.

"The one with the policy on Holly's life."

"I didn't know she had one."

"I'll bet Sully did," Paul said. "Five hundred thousand dollars in the case of accidental death, but they won't pay if Sully murdered her."

"Or if it were a suicide."

"You shut your mouth, Joth."

Paul took another deep breath.

"What did you tell him, Paul? The insurance guy, I mean."

"Nothing yet. And I don't plan to talk to him, if Sully cooperates."

"What's that mean?" I said.

Paul's face was getting redder.

"It's justice," he said. "You ask Sully to take any kind of responsibility; you ask him to pay for the funeral, and he says he left Holly six years ago. But the house? That's a different story. When it's the property we're talking about, he's still her husband."

"And that's why it's his property."

"All he has to do is sign it over," said Paul.

"Or?"

"If he doesn't, I'm going to start talking."

Paul swayed a bit. He could never hold his liquor, even back in college, and unlike Sully he could be a nasty drunk.

"You don't want to open up that can of worms," I said.

"Why not?"

"Let it play out, Paul. Holly had a will, so let the courts decide what to do with her assets."

"So you are representing him?"

"I'm hoping there won't be anything to represent him on."

"You have to choose a side, Joth."

Paul had grown animated and a crowd had begun to develop around us. When he noticed, he reacted with embarrassment. He broke away and headed right for Sully, catching up to him near the bar. I trailed after him but not fast enough.

"You got a lot of nerve being here," Paul said.

He grabbed Sully by the shoulder, apparently forgetting that it was Sully who had organized the wake.

"You killed her, you son of a bitch. You see what she looks like in death? You see what you did to her, Sully?"

Now I understood that it was Paul who had insisted on an open coffin. He wanted everyone to blame Sully in public for what had become of his once-vivacious sister.

Then Sully declared the one thing he shouldn't have said.

"I was her husband."

Paul wasn't much of a midfielder, but he could hit. He laid Sully out with one punch to the jaw. Sully, with a few too many drinks in him, too, never saw it coming.

While friends pulled Paul away, I got Sully to his feet and helped him out to the vestibule where I found him a seat on an upholstered couch.

"You okay?"

As Sully rubbed the side of his jaw, I saw that he was still wobbly, but that was more because of the whiskey than the punch.

"I'm all right."

"I'm gonna take you home, okay?"

"That's probably a good idea."

Then Sully yelled across the room to Paul, as if they were still settling a score at the end of a frat party.

"You clean this mess up, Paul. And send me the bill, you punk."

I got him out of there as fast as I could.

Sully had a long history of acting against his lawyer's advice. As usual, he had ignored my sensible guidance, and I couldn't resist the self-serving impulse to tell him so on the drive home. He rubbed his jaw and told me to shut up, and for once I didn't blame him for saying so.

About halfway home he spoke again, his voice sullen and distorted by his swelling jaw.

"That goddamn bitch was asking Paul about my interest in the property."

It took me a moment to identify the subject of this attack.

"Heather?"

"What do you think they were talking about?"

I didn't believe it. The coroner had already reached his conclusion. Besides, Heather would never violate the social mores of a friend's wake to further an investigation of a member of the family. At least, I didn't think she would.

"Who told you that, Sully?"

"You know what the problem with you is, Joth? You don't pay attention."

"Really?"

"You know what he told her?"

"I have no idea, Sully. I don't think you do either."

"Riley told me. He overheard the whole thing. She thinks I had a motive."

"You don't think maybe somebody dropped that piece of information just to get under your skin?"

Although I was thinking of Riley, I knew that Sully would assume I meant Paul, but it didn't matter.

"Well, it's working," he said, still rubbing his jaw.

"I can see that."

I pulled up in front of his house. There were no other cars in the driveway or on the street.

"Lori around?"

"Doesn't look like it."

I waited for more. Sully was slowing down.

"She got transferred to an office in Crystal City."

"Are you still seeing her?"

"She doesn't like the commute from here, that's all."

Sully pushed open the car door with some extra effort and I helped him inside. Crystal City was an easier commute than D.C.

"She can get to Crystal City on the Metro."

"Well, I know that, but she's got herself a little blue Mini-Cooper and she likes to drive it. So that's it."

"You broke up?"

Sully looked unsteady standing there in his living room.

"Yeah."

"When?"

"None of your damn business."

I managed to get him into his Barcalounger and helped him put his feet up.

"You could do worse, Sully."

He didn't like me commenting on his personal life and took a cheap shot to prove it.

"And you could have done worse than Heather. Looks like you did."

"Let me get some ice for your jaw."

I made my way to the kitchen.

"And a drink wouldn't hurt either," he said.

"Way ahead of you, pal."

I found a half-empty fifth of bourbon in a cabinet and poured us each a couple of shots over ice. I found a plastic storage bag in a kitchen drawer and dumped the rest of the ice from the freezer into it.

"You've got to forget about Paul," I said as I handed him the bag.

Sully took a deep breath, placed the ice bag against his jaw, and winced.

"Valium. That stuff's easy to come by, Joth. I told you that. I'll bet half of Congress is on it."

"Well, that would explain a lot of things."

"Heather knows that."

"Let it go, Sully."

"What about this insurance angle?"

I was surprised it had taken him so long to come around to the financial issue. "You had a life insurance policy on her?"

"No. She took one out herself years ago in case something happened. So it turns out she wasn't so dumb after all."

He put the ice bag down and rested the cocktail glass against his jaw. He had a pretty good bruise developing already on the left side of his face.

"Man, he popped me pretty good."

"He did . . . and he's capable of worse. "I haven't seen the policy, Sully," I continued, "but I suspect Paul's right. It'll pay for an accidental death, but not if she killed herself. Or if the beneficiary killed her."

Sully laughed grimly and it looked like it hurt his face.

"I doubt I'm the beneficiary, Joth."

"Yeah," I said, "but your kids are. That means you don't have to go into your own pocket to send them to college."

"You've got the answer for everything, don't you?"

"I won't be the only person reaching that conclusion."

"You think Paul's going to argue that I killed his sister if it keeps me from sending his niece and nephew to college?"

I considered it for a second and concluded that only a guy like Paul was enough of a self-absorbed mercenary to tarnish his sister's memory for a chance to screw his ex-brother-in-law.

"You know him better than me."

Sully looked at me and waited for the rest of it.

"Let's assume he really thinks you killed her. He may figure your old friend won't prosecute you for murder."

"You mean *can't* prosecute me for murder."

I shrugged and nodded.

"That, too."

I turned it over in my mind, but Sully finished his thought before I finished mine.

"It's all about the property, Joth; you know that. All of this—the laptop, the insurance—it's all about the property."

"Is it worth that much to him?"

"Let's face it, Joth, he and I are both down on our luck. The guy who develops that property is going to be a wealthy man."

"There's enough there to make you both comfortable."

"There's nothing comfortable about partnering with a guy who's ready to blackmail you."

Sully had a fair point.

"What about the laptop?"

"I have it, so what?"

I figured Sully did, but I didn't think he'd admit it. He was drunker than I thought. "Can I see it?"

"No."

"You realize you're withholding evidence of a crime?"

"There wasn't any crime, Joth. Can't you get that through your thick head? She died the way she lived and I'm truly sorry about that."

"There was a crime for sure if she were blackmailing George Duggan. Or Jimmie Flambeau."

"Nobody in their right mind would try to blackmail Jimmie Flambeau unless they wanted to end up at the bottom of the Potomac River."

"What about Duggan?"

"I said I wasn't sure about him."

Sully put the ice bag back against his jaw.

"I just know there was some dirty business going on."

"How do you know that?"

He hedged for a minute, rubbing his jaw to buy some time.

"Got to be," Sully said. "What else makes sense?

"Why can't this just be a business deal?" I said.

By that point, I was getting exasperated.

"The property's a developer's dream, Sully. Why don't you put your grudges aside and cut in those people you need to keep happy?"

"Because Paul wouldn't do business with Duggan."

"Are you thinking about working with him?"

"Of course not. Look, Joth, there are things you don't know.

"Maybe I need to, Sully."

"I don't need this kind of thing to get out, all right?"

"You mean, it's just talk?"

"I mean those are dangerous people."

"Who?"

Sully abruptly changed his posture and his tone.

"Look, if Holly was blackmailing anybody, that's her crime, and she's dead. Anyway, who's to say the laptop's hers? I paid for it."

"You bought her a laptop?"

"I bought myself a laptop."

"Let's get back to the other point, Sully. Were you planning to develop the property with Paul?"

The drink and the punch had weakened his resolve and with a grumble he gave in.

"The fact is, there was talk about it."

I waited for more.

"About four or five months ago, Paul finally figured out that I didn't have any ownership interest in it."

"Why would he have thought otherwise?"

"Well, I may have told him that Holly and I owned it jointly."

"I see."

"When he found out Holly still had sole title, he started pressuring her. He was going to develop it and cut me out."

"Develop it with who, if not Duggan?"

Sully shrugged and grimaced.

"I heard some names come up."

"And Duggan was one of them?"

"Duggan ruined me and Holly, too. Paul hated Duggan as much as I do."

"But he knows the business. He's a developer. He has fewer costs."

"Point is, they were going to cut me out."

"They?"

"Obviously I'm not real excited about Heather knowing that. But now you understand why I don't want to do business with that bullet-headed son of a bitch."

I let the facts seep into my mind for a few seconds.

"How are you going to develop it?"

"Not with Duggan, I can tell you that."

"You haven't prepared a subdivision plan. Do you even know if it percs?"

"Percs? What are you talking about?"

Beyond the reach of the sewer system, real property couldn't be developed in Arlington unless ground water tests demonstrated that the land would percolate.

I rolled my eyes at Sully, wondering how in the world he could pull this off.

"I thought that was the first thing real estate developers did. Run a perc test. If the property doesn't drain sufficiently to support a septic field, you're out of luck."

A blank look came over his face.

"You don't know, do you, Sully?

"Of course it percs. There's a house on it now."

"The house predates the current land use rules, you idiot. And you're talking about subdividing it."

"It percs, Joth, goddammit. Don't you worry about it."

That was his story and he was sticking to it.

"Duggan will insist on a perc test," I said.

"I told you, I don't need Duggan," Sully said.

He sounded as defiant as ever.

"Whoever owns that property is going to make money, and that someone is me."

Chapter Ten

Paul Turns the Screws

Holly's funeral was not as well-attended as her wake, probably because no free food or drinks were provided. It was held at St. Carolyn's Catholic Church in Arlington, beginning with a traditional funeral Mass without frills, conducted by Father John Tedesco. The service was as quick and grim as Father John himself. He gave the urn containing Holly's ashes to her daughter Sarah and that was it. The two dozen or so of us in attendance filed out into a morning of cold spring rain.

As I stood under the portico waiting for a break in the downpour, Dave Sullivan came outside and stood next to me. It had been several years since I'd spoken to my godson, so long that I barely recognized him. His taciturn features and the circles under his eyes showed how hard his mother's death had hit him.

"Hey, Dave. Been a long time."

He raised his eyes and fixed me with a cold expression that he held for a beat longer than necessary before extending his hand in polite deference.

"Mr. Proctor," he said.

He had grown to be a big kid, solid like his uncle but taller, with a strong, affirmative handshake.

"I'm awful sorry about your mom."

Dave looked at me blankly, nodded his head and looked away, but he made no move to leave the portico. Then he turned back to me as if he'd reached a conclusion.

"I saw you kneeling at the prayer rail at the wake."

"Yes," I said. "That was me."

I remembered my rote performance, which at least matched and possibly exceeded Father John's perfunctory delivery of the funeral Mass.

"You think that's going to do any good?" said Dave.

"I hope so," I said.

I was coming up empty in my search for comforting words.

Dave looked at me and his face seemed to soften for just a moment.

"I don't feel that way, Mr. Proctor. I wish I did, but I just don't."

The role of godfather comes with responsibilities, and as our eyes met, I understood that I had performed those duties with the same lack of commitment I had brought to every other personal obligation I had ever undertaken in my adult life. For a moment, I felt sorrier for myself than I did for my godson. I didn't know where to begin.

"Do you have a ride?"

"I'm with my dad, but who knows where he is?"

"Come on, I'll give you a ride."

Dave hesitated as if he were making a choice between two forms of punishment. Then, without saying anything else, he came with me.

Traffic was light, but conditions were awful, and I let the silence continue, focusing my full attention on the traffic and the road.

"This is a bunch of shit, isn't it?" Dave said, breaking our silence.

"Yeah," I said. "It is."

"How would you know?"

"Because my mom died when I was about your age."

After a while, he decided to ask me about it.

"How'd she die?"

"Cancer."

"Take a long time?"

"Yeah, it did."

"My mom had been dying for a long time, too."

"I'm not quite sure what you mean by that," I said.

Dave spoke quietly but without emotion, as if he were talking about some other person's mother.

"The drinking, the drugs, you know. It's like she had been waiting to die."

"Since your dad left?"

"No," Dave said.

As he changed his posture, I felt him shift into a more introspective mindset.

"Men have always disappointed her," he said, "and I'm sure I'm one of them."

"Nonsense, Dave. You got into UVA."

"That's not the point. Not at all. I'll come out all right; I know that. But look at all the men who came through her life: Dad, Uncle Paul, Mr. Duggan. They've all got their own angle and they're all in it for themselves. They all tried to use Mom to help them get where they wanted to go. She saw that, but she just couldn't do anything about it, except take what they gave her and make the best of it."

I looked across at him and nodded.

"It was a shitty little life she had that way," he said. "And you know what? She deserved better."

I let that sit a second.

"How's your sister doing?"

"Not well. She's caught in the middle. Just like our mom was always caught in the middle."

I thought about the Sarah I remembered: sweet, fragile and naive. She was in for a rough time, and I hoped Sully was prepared for that.

"Did you know Mr. Duggan well?" I said.

Dave shrugged away the discomfort that crossed his face.

"I wish I'd never met the guy. I wish none of us had."

"But what about your mom?"

"My mom hated him."

He glanced across at me.

"You didn't know my mom as well as you think. She liked the taste of revenge and there wasn't much she wouldn't do to get it."

That took me a while to digest before I answered.

"She paid a big price for it, didn't she, Dave?"

"She was always paying a price for something. I think it just got to the point where she couldn't keep track of her grudges. I like to think she was finally past all that, but I don't know."

I pulled into the driveway. We sat for a moment, listening to the rain fall on the windshield, as I wondered what I could say to help.

"You believe in God, Mr. Proctor?"

"Sure," I said, with what I hoped was a trace of conviction.

"Well, I don't know about the afterlife," said Dave, "but one of these days, we'll see if there's any justice on this earth."

"Dave, what would justice look like in this case?"

He looked over at me and smiled.

"Thanks for the ride, Mr. Proctor."

Dave stepped out into the rain. He got me on that one.

On Monday morning I got to the office early, but Paul was already there. As I poured myself a cup of coffee, Marie casually mentioned that my client had arrived for his appointment and had asked to wait in my office.

I didn't have an appointment on my calendar. I asked her to describe him and when she did, I felt a surge of disgust.

"A heavyset, bald-headed man," she said.

I could hear him prowling around in there as I approached the closed door. I threw it open suddenly and caught him behind my desk, snooping around among my papers.

"I ought to throw you out on your ear."

"You and whose army?"

"For such a crusader after justice, Paul, you don't seem to care too much about the common courtesies of our society."

I knew he was unmoved by this, but he gave me a chastened expression, then moved around and took a seat in one of the client chairs.

"You're right and I'm sorry. I've got no business nosing around."

I began straightening up the papers on my desk.

"Except that you'd do it again if you had the chance. Well, let me tell you something: Don't."

"You think you can talk to me like that?"

"If you don't like it, leave. I didn't invite you here."

Paul slumped. Whatever it was he was cooking up, he knew he was going to have to persuade me of his good faith in order to obtain my cooperation. He started laying out the standard excuses.

"Look, Joth, I'm sorry. My sister's dead and I'm under a lot of stress."

"Undoubtedly."

The chill in my tone drew an immediate grumble.

"I've got responsibility for her kids, you know."

"They've still got a father, Paul."

"Hell of a role model, he is."

"And Dave's an adult. He can make his own decisions."

I was wondering where all this would leave Sarah.

Paul shuffled in his chair. He was already scheming.

"I'm willing to make a deal."

"What a surprise."

"I've got a property that backs up on Rock Spring Park. Arts-and-Craft style house in a great neighborhood. Three bedrooms, two-and-a-half baths. More than he needs. I'm willing to work a swap."

"And what makes you so generous?"

He sighed, looked out the window and his body sagged. He wasn't likely to con me and he knew it, and he also knew that he'd never wear Sully down. He was tired of the fight, especially now that he'd lost his sister.

"Look, Joth, we go back a long way. You taught me everything I knew about running midfield. I never would have made the team if it wasn't for you."

"I hope I taught you more than that."

"You did. I looked up to you. You were smart and successful."

"So get to the point."

"I trust you. I trust your judgment. Sully might not admit it, but he does, too. This family squabble is getting out of hand. What I'm asking for is fair. It's right. And I think you know it is, too."

He gave me the address of the house.

"There's a realtor's lockbox with a key inside on the door handle. The combination's my birthday: November 18. 11-18. That's it. Take Sully over there and show him the house. He'll love it. He'll listen to you, Joth."

I folded my hands and looked carefully at him. For all his size and muscle, he was just a little bit afraid of something. It wasn't me and it wasn't Sully.

"Are you really ready to develop that property, Paul?"

"Absolutely. I've got financing all lined up."

"Subdivision plan?"

"It's in the works."

I remembered my last discussion with Sully.

"Do you know if it percs?"

"Sure," Paul said. "Ask Sully."

"You ran a test?"

"Didn't need to. There's a house on it."

He was echoing Sully's line.

"All right. I'll see what he says. What if he says no?"

Paul's combative expression returned to his face in an instant.

"I know it'll be tough to prove he killed her. You have to prove murder beyond a reasonable doubt, and there are too many other possibilities."

"Did Heather tell you that?"

"I watch TV. I'm not stupid, Joth. But the insurance is different."

Paul seemed to be waiting for me to respond, and when I didn't, he continued.

"You think the insurance company wants to write Sully a half-million-dollar check? All they have to do is be persuaded that it's more likely than not that she was killed or that she killed herself. They'll deny coverage and he'll get nothing."

That was the argument of a desperate or deranged man.

"Paul, you're not going to tell an insurance company that your beloved sister killed herself so you can deny your nephew a college education."

He didn't reply and so my point was made.

"Just talk to him," Paul said. "What I'm offering is a win-win. Sully's a businessman. He's got to like that."

Paul was also a businessman, but he did not understand people or their motivations, and it was that blind spot that had kept him from any significant success. The deal held a certain attraction, but Sully would never go for it.

"What you don't seem to understand, Paul, is that Sully is nothing if not stubborn. You could offer him Windsor Castle and he wouldn't take it if he thought you were threatening him."

"I know that. I should have thought of that before. I screwed up, and that's why I'm here. But you can talk to him, Joth. You can make it happen."

"Maybe."

I got up and started walking toward the door. Paul took the hint and stood up.

"You can, you know. He'll listen to you, Joth. He always has."

"I might. We'll see."

I held the door open. Paul stepped through and held out his hand.

"I'll let you know," I said, as I shut the door in his face.

After trying to avoid it for several hours, I dropped by the courthouse to do some perfunctory legal research in the bar association library. Half an hour later, I gave in and took the elevator upstairs. Betty admitted that Heather was in her office before checking with her. I think that was the only reason she invited me in.

"What is it this time?" she said.

She was standing at a table working through some files and didn't look up.

"Looks like you're busy."

"I've got a trial tomorrow."

I took the hint and didn't sit down.

"I didn't think you tried cases anymore, now that you're the top dog."

She slapped a file shut and spun around to stare at me.

"Big cases, Joth. Murders, things like that. What can I do for you?"

"It's about Sully," I said.

"Is it?"

"I take that as a retraction of your offer of a drink."

"What offer?" she said.

My upper lip moved between my teeth and I nodded.

"I just want to get some closure on Sully. I assume your office might be . . ."

"Don't assume anything."

"Fair enough, Heather. I just want to know."

"If you're asking me if I think Sully killed his wife, the answer is yes."

I'd had enough, and my temper rose to match hers.

"Then why's he walking around free?"

"Believing it is not the same as proving it, but don't think we're done trying."

Something had changed since the last time we talked, and I didn't think it was my refusal of the drink offer. She'd been talking to someone, or someone had been talking to her. Either way, we were in new territory.

"Fine," I said.

I spun on my heel to leave.

"He's got a laptop that belonged to his wife, and I want it."

I turned right back.

"I don't think he does."

"You heard me, Joth. He better come up with it or we'll see what a grand jury thinks about all this."

"All this what?" I said.

I was sparring now because her insistence on the laptop already seemed to provide the answer.

"Heather, is Paul's persistance wearing you down?"

Her already stern and combative expression hardened.

"What's he doing for work?" she said.

"Who, Sully?"

As far as I knew, Sully wasn't doing anything for work.

"He's got a consulting business," I said. "You know that. Nothing's changed."

"He's waiting for an insurance payoff," she said.

So Paul had tried that angle with Heather, too.

"Sounds like you already have all the answers, Heather."

"I want that laptop," she said.

I turned around and left her office, grabbing my phone as I did. When several calls to Sully's number went unanswered, I got in the car. He was at home, or rather, he was at Riley's late mother's house, when I got there. He was watching the Caps game on a big-screen, high definition TV. I saw a bottle of rum and a half-empty tumbler on the coffee table. Sully offered me a glass and I shook my head. The big, comfortably furnished room was as cluttered as a fraternity house basement.

"Riley's been pretty generous about the rent, huh?" I said.

It was an unnecessarily provocative comment and Sully tilted his head to consider my expression.

"All my friends are generous, Joth. I've been unusually blessed."

Sully delivered this encomium in the usual flat tone he adopted whenever he wanted to tinge his sarcasm with ambiguity.

"I wonder if you even know who your friends are anymore, Sully."

He flashed a comfortable smile.

"The only one I'm sure of is you," he said.

The swelling in his jaw had gone down, but he still had a pretty good bruise where Paul's punch had landed. He nodded his head and waited.

"So Paul thinks . . ."

"It doesn't matter what Paul thinks," Sully said.

"Yeah, it does," I said. "And that goes double with Heather."

"The hell with Heather."

"I wouldn't trifle with her if I were you," I said. "She's more open with me than you are and you're my client. Now why is that?"

" 'Cause I never slept with you."

I stifled an impulse to bruise the other side of his jaw.

"You're going out of your way to piss people off, Sully. Do you think everyone's out to get you? Or do you have something you're making sure stays hidden?"

"You worried about getting paid?"

"Now that you mention it."

"When things turn around, Joth, I'll pay you. Riley, too. He knows that. Besides, you got anything else to do?"

It was a fact of our long-standing relationship that he could slap me with the sort of insult that had cost him so many of his old friends. I guess I stubbornly stuck around because I knew I was the last one he had.

"I saw Heather today."

A few too many drinks had made Sully logy and he was unmoved.

"What a surprise."

"She told me she thinks you killed your wife."

"Are we back to that again? Holly died of an accidental drug overdose. What could be more obvious?"

"You want a grand jury answering that question?"

135

Sully finished swirling his drink, drained what was left of it and put the glass on the coffee table.

"No," he said.

He actually sounded chastened.

"You think any of this is easy for me, Joth. I loved her once. We had two kids. Okay, it didn't work out. That happens. Now tell me what Heather really wants."

"She wants the laptop."

"Do you know why?" he said.

I still didn't know, but that didn't keep me from speculating.

"Because Paul's convinced her that there's evidence of some sort of deal on there. Something to support his claim on the property. Is there?"

"No."

"Then why not give it to her?"

"Because it's my goddamn laptop. There are personal things on there and there's no evidence of any crime because no crime's been committed."

"Paul doesn't care if you get prosecuted, Sully, and he doesn't want to sue you. He just wants the property."

"Exactly. He's trying to shake me down for the property and he's gotten Heather to buy into this crazy laptop scheme. He knows I'm ready to develop it without him, so he says there's stuff on Holly's laptop that would reveal some sort of juicy conspiracy that Heather could sink her fangs into. That's just the kind of thing that would make her cute little ears prick up. I understand all that, but I get the property and there's nothing they can do about that."

I took a moment to take all of that in.

"What's on that laptop that you don't want Heather to see?"

"It's my goddamn laptop."

"She doesn't owe you anything, Sully. You know that."

"We're old friends."

"As far as she's concerned, you're a crook who got away with it last time."

"I'm not worried about it, Joth. Heather will let you know before she gets ready to turn this over to a grand jury."

I had to wonder about that.

"How many houses do you think a developer could put up on that property?" I said. "How many of those McMansions that go for seven figures each?"

"I can do the same thing, Joth."

"Can you?"

I considered dropping George Duggan's name, but Sully and I were already on edge with each other.

"You don't know anything about developing property, Sully. You don't even know what a perc test is. You'd have to team up with someone."

"There are plenty of developers who'll stand in line for a piece of that deal."

"Listen to me. There's too much money at stake for Paul to roll over. He's already making trouble for you. He's got a property not too far from there."

"So?"

"He's got a proposition for you, Sully."

"A proposition, huh? I don't like it already."

But he did. Sully was pleased at himself for pushing Paul into a corner.

"Naturally," I said.

"But you think I should hear what you have to say."

"I think that would be wise," I said. "And so do you."

Sully was being stubborn, but he had a scent for the deal and for Paul's desperation to make it.

"Okay, let's have it."

"It's a nice Arts-and-Crafts style house. Backs up on Rock Spring Park and a pretty stream. Wooded lot. I'm sure Paul would work a trade."

"Not with me, he won't."

"Three bedrooms, Sully, with two and a half baths."

"Three bedrooms, huh? Not interested."

"It's an upscale neighborhood."

"It's one lot."

"Paul's a businessman."

"He's a son of a bitch."

"It's just numbers, Sully. I think there's a deal to be made."

"He wants me to be charged with murdering my wife. He's threatened my kids' insurance payout. There's nothing he can say that scares me. I'm not making a deal. I'm developing the property."

"What about the laptop?"

Sully laughed.

"Tell Heather I get the message."

He was right about a number of things. For one, if the laptop really was his, then he had no obligation to give it to her.

"You have a receipt for it?" I said.

"You think I can lay my hands on it in this dump?"

I started losing patience.

"You're determined to do this the hard way, aren't you, Sully?"

He leaned his head against the back of the chair and laughed like a man who'd had one drink too many, which he'd probably had.

"When people start pushing, you have to push back. That's the way it is, Joth. You taught me that. Tell her what I told you. I've got nothing that belongs to Holly. That'll shut her up."

Sully got up and went to the kitchen for more Coke and ice. When he came back, I didn't waste any time asking him what I needed to know.

"What exactly do you want me to do, Sully?"

"I want you to fix it," he said.

"Is that what I am to you? A fixer?"

"Yeah," Sully said. "So like you did with the Duggan mess. Just fix it."

Chapter Eleven

An Old Flame Chimes In

On a brisk but sunny late morning in early spring, I walked two blocks to the office of Hillman and Garfield, a domestic relations boutique firm on the top floor of a four-story office building near the courthouse.

I'd known Liz Hillman for a long time. Like Heather Burke and me, she'd been a member of the Arlington Bar back when it was a small, collegial club. I was dating Liz when I met Heather. I dropped her rather unceremoniously, and though she'd gone out of her way to remain civil ever since, I knew she'd exact her revenge if the opportunity arose. I couldn't blame her. I probably deserved whatever comeuppance she had in store for me.

I waited for Liz in a lobby that also served as the firm's law library, a rectangular room with shelves of law books on three walls. Along the fourth wall, windows faced the verdant and semi-developed landscape of North Arlington. Not a bad view.

Liz was the same age as Heather, but she looked older now than her years. A petite woman with auburn hair, she had developed a tough, leathery complexion, the product of a two-pack-a-day habit that stretched back decades.

"Joth," she said, with a warm smile. "To what do I owe this nice surprise?"

"Don't we have a lunch date today?"

My question seemed to stump her for a moment and then she laughed.

"I should be so lucky."

"Do you have other plans?"

Liz was a savvy veteran of the domestic relations wars and she could smell a conspiracy a mile away. She also couldn't resist one.

"As a matter of fact, Joth, I don't."

"There's that Thai place on the plaza you used to like."

"It's still there."

"Yeah, I know. I made a reservation."

She smiled again and shook her head. If I had been paying closer attention, I might have thought she was flirting with me, but my mind was elsewhere, wondering what information she might have for me.

We took the elevator to the building lobby and, as we headed to the exit, Liz took an unfiltered cigarette from her purse and had it lit as soon as she got one foot out the door. We were almost across the street before she gave in to the silence.

"One of my clients died last week," she said.

I nodded.

"Holly Sullivan," I said. "I thought I was going to see you at the wake."

A fleeting expression of guilt passed across Liz's face. Where she once seemed so lovely, she now appeared locked into a stern, almost bitter appearance.

"I would like to have been there," she said, "but unfortunately I had a client drop in unexpectedly."

I brushed this lie aside with a shrug.

"It's a sad thing to see a woman die that young."

"What did she die of?"

Liz had to know the answer to that question. I assumed she was fishing for the reason I'd come looking for her.

"Accidental drug overdose," I said, "at least according to the coroner's report."

The cherry trees that lined the plaza behind the government office building on Clarendon were budding nicely, and their limbs trembled in the breeze. The decorative wrought iron benches were full of men in cardigan sweaters and women in wool skirts, reading paperbacks or lost on their iPhones. Busboys were setting up tables outside restaurants for hearty or adventurous diners, eager to brave the chilly air for a chance to take in the change of season and be seen in a trendy place.

"How's your practice, Joth?" Liz said.

She asked this with the solicitude of a doctor regarding an aging patient. Then again, at least she asked.

"Pretty good. Ups and downs, as you know."

"I don't see you around the bar functions like I used to," she said, between puffs. "That's where business gets done, you know."

"Just got out of the habit, I guess."

"Still doing criminal law?" I said.

"Yeah, you know it. That and the dogs and cats my old friends send my way."

I held open the door of the restaurant for her while she stubbed out her cigarette in the sand-filled receptacle just inside it. The noon hour rush hadn't yet begun, so we were conveniently ahead of the crowd. We walked up two steps and were immediately seated. Liz took a quick look at her menu, ordered, and folded it in front of her.

"This meeting wouldn't have anything to do with Holly, would it?"

I had a glib response ready, but I saw by her expression that she expected frankness. I ordered the Pad Thai and turned to Liz.

"I'm afraid it does."

"What do you want to know, Joth?"

"I'm not sure what the status of the attorney-client privilege is, she being dead and all, but I need to know a little about Holly's divorce case."

"I see."

Liz sat back in her chair and eyed me with curiosity. The first two fingers of her right hand went to the double strand of pearls around her neck and she began fingering them like a rosary. I wanted something from her, and I could see her gaming her response.

I suddenly felt tired. I rubbed my eyes and pinched the bridge of my nose with a thumb and forefinger.

"I represent Sully. It's an unattended death, but that's not really the issue."

"Okay," she said impatiently. "So what is it?"

"I need to know the status of the property settlement between them."

"I can't tell you anything about that," she said.

"I understand the estate might still have claims. I'm guessing Holly's brother Paul will qualify as executor and that the matter will be up to him. That's all for another day."

I straightened up and put my hands on the table as I leaned in a little toward Liz.

"The only thing I really want to know is, was there any understanding between Sully and Holly on the family residence up there off North Glebe Road?"

It took Liz a long time to answer. She put her weathered chin in her hand, rested her elbow on the table and studied me. She didn't have much of a reputation for strict adherence to ethical strictures, but she was a bulldog of an advocate for her clients. I didn't expect to get much information from her during our lunch.

"There was no understanding between them about much of anything," she said.

"That's what Sully says."

Liz's expression narrowed and her voice took on an edge.

"That was Holly's family property and they're entitled to it."

"And they'll get it, Liz. Maybe Paul won't, but whatever profits Sully realizes will end up in the kids' hands."

"That wasn't the way Holly wanted it," Liz said.

She sounded pretty insistent, which I noted for future reference.

"How did Holly want it, then?" I said.

"She was sentimentally attached to that property."

Although Sully had always kept his wife insulated from mundane financial matters, Holly had an instinct for picking up nuggets of information that might be useful to her someday. I wouldn't have been surprised if she didn't know what bank they used, but the sentimentality argument was a fig leaf.

"Liz," I said, "they're going to develop the property either way. The only question is, who ends up getting the money? Whoever told you it's about maintaining the family homestead is uh . . ."

"What?"

"They're deceiving you."

Liz laughed off the idea that she could be deceived by anyone, but her eyes glazed over for a moment, and I watched her turn over the facts in her mind. She seemed to feel a commensurate obligation to enlighten me a bit and leaned in a little to make sure I heard every word.

"Well, Joth, let me tell you something. Holly wanted Paul to get the property."

I peered a little closer at Liz to be sure she meant it.

"Instead of her own kids, which would be the case if Sully develops it?"

"I don't think she thought it through that far."

I wondered if Liz Hillman was the one who hadn't thought it through that far, or if she had finally found a way to exact her pound of flesh from me. I let her comment go, smiled and asked her about her family. Our food came and we talked of old friends and the many changes in the face of Arlington County.

After I paid for lunch, I walked Liz back to her office while she inhaled another smoke. We stopped on the sidewalk in front of her building, and I gave her time to finish the cigarette. She seemed to appreciate the gesture.

"Sully said Holly was pushing hard for the divorce just before she died," I said.

It wasn't true, but I was hoping to goad Liz into an unguarded response.

"Joth, let me tell you something else about Holly and Sully, something you probably don't know. That case languished for years because she never really wanted the divorce. Did you know that?"

"Is that why they never came up with a property settlement agreement?"

Liz nodded.

"Holly understood that making that move would be the first step on the path to the end. She didn't want that."

"She thought he'd take her back?"

"Hoped."

Her expression turned ruefully, as if she were sharing the same feeling.

"Holly loved and admired her husband, and she knew her kids needed a father. She always hoped he'd come back. But I know for a fact that she wanted Paul to have the property. She told me that in no uncertain terms the last time I talked to her."

"When was that?"

"Less than a week before she died. I don't know the exact date."

I turned that over in my head.

"Does Heather know that?"

Liz finished the cigarette and nodded through a vigorous coughing jag.

"Of course."

"I suppose you think Sully should do the right thing and renounce his claim on the property?"

Her expression revealed exasperation at my apparent naïveté.

"It's not that easy," she said. "We can't always get what we want, Joth. Fact is, Sully owns the property. If he transfers it now, it's a taxable event. So no, that's between the men. And you make a good point, Joth. Holly's kids will get the benefit either way."

"One would think," I said.

Liz glanced up curiously at me.

"One would think," she said.

"Liz," I said, "knowing Holly wanted to cut Sully out . . ."

"No, I don't think Sully did anything that led to her death."

Liz interrupted me delicately and I could see that she assumed that this was my real question.

"I'd bet my house against it," she said. "Not over a piece of property. Deep down, he really cared about her, Joth."

"Did you tell Heather that, too?"

"Yes, I did."

I shook her hand and a smile lit up her face.

"We need to do this more often," she said.

That was true. The business I was in required it.

"You're right," I said. "And we will."

When I returned to my office, I picked up the phone and called Paul Saunders on his cell phone. By the sound of it, he was outside when he answered. I heard birds and the whoosh of a garden hose.

"You playing golf, Paul?"

He recognized my voice.

"Working, Joth. What's on your mind?"

He sounded typically impatient.

"Looking at developing a lot off North Glebe, maybe?" I said.

"I don't own a lot off North Glebe," Paul said. "You told me that yourself."

"Well, I have some bad news for you, then, Paul. Sully's not interested in the swap you proposed."

He sniffed.

"Has he got a counter?"

"No, no counteroffer. He just said he wasn't interested."

That was intended as a kiss-off and Paul knew it. I could almost hear his teeth grind.

"He's making a mistake, Joth."

"He's a big boy."

"Not as big as he thinks."

"Oh, and about the laptop, Paul. There wasn't one. At least not one that belonged to your sister."

I expected pushback and I was surprised when I didn't get any.

"I don't care about the laptop, Joth. What I care about is the family property."

"I told you what he said."

Paul swore, which seemed to come naturally to him.

"Holly wanted it to come to me so I could develop it for the kids."

"Yeah, it had great sentimental value to her," I said.

I tried to reply with all the sarcasm I could muster. Paul was making the same point Liz Hillman had, which proved nothing except that he and Liz had been talking.

"Cut the crap, Joth. We both know what this is about. I can develop the property and Sully can't. I'm willing to cut him in for a fair percentage. I've told you that again and again. But I'm the developer. He needs me. End of story."

He was already bidding against himself.

"Okay, Paul, so that's your price? Control of the project?"

"That's my price."

"I know what that means," I said. "It means you hire your own development company. You pay yourself exorbitant development fees and consulting fees and engineering fees and Sully's left with a meager percentage of what's not eaten up by you."

"That's not true, Joth, and you know it. Sully will have a say in all the costs. We'll put a cap on expenses if he wants. Or I'll give him a minimum guarantee. I'll give him consulting fees that match my own."

Paul was running on like a teenage girl with a new crush.

"You've thought a lot about this, haven't you?"

I heard him take in his breath and reassess.

"Time is of the essence, Joth. This is prime North Arlington real estate, a stone's throw from Chain Bridge, ten minutes from Georgetown. It would be irresponsible of me to let it sit here."

"You need the money that badly?"

The question seemed to offend him.

"I don't need the money. It's Sully who needs the money. He has kids to educate. I'm doing him a favor."

There was nothing else to say; no other angle to pursue with him. I wanted to explain to Paul that his approach was all wrong, that Sully could sense an over-eager trade partner the way a doctor could sense an illness. It didn't help that Sully didn't like Paul or respect him. In fact, he was quite willing to drag him around by the nose just for the sadistic pleasure it gave him. They'd make the deal sooner or later, but not before Sully tied Paul up in knots.

Several days later, after getting a client's DWI reduced to a charge of Reckless Driving, I took the elevator to the sixth floor, where I waited half an hour for Heather to see me. I had nothing new to discuss. I just wanted to see if her attitude had changed. Or maybe I just wanted to see her. That was always a possibility.

I was sensitive to the tinge of resentment that carried over from our last conversation, but Paul's example wasn't lost on me. I couldn't let Heather manipulate me the way Sully was toying with Paul. Once inside, I challenged her before I even sat down.

"I assume you're closing the file on Holly Sullivan."

Heather rocked in her chair before replying. She didn't get her job because she rattled easily.

"What makes you think that, Joth?"

"Come on, Heather. You saw the coroner's report," I said. "You brought it up at the wake."

"He's the coroner. I'm the Commonwealth Attorney."

"And there's no laptop."

"Sully told you that, huh?"

"You know there's no laptop. By now, I'm sure you've checked sales receipts at every vendor in northern Virginia."

"You're not a lawyer anymore, Joth. You know what you are? You're just a fixer. People hire you to patch up the broken pieces when a plan goes bad. And you go bad right along with it."

I sensed something different in her tone and manner. During our previous meeting, Heather had displayed a professional impatience that came with the territory. This personal assault showed something else—a hostility borne of a deeper anxiety, and if I had been forced to admit it, it stung a bit.

"Plan?" I said. "Sully never planned anything in his life. That's his problem."

"Why don't you bring him into my office?" she said. "It's about time he and I had a little chat."

I pushed right back.

"You going to give him immunity?"

"What's he got to say that would cause me to offer him immunity?"

"Why would he talk to you without it, Heather, unless he's not a suspect?"

"Suspect in what?"

That was going nowhere, and I knew I had to pivot.

"Has Paul been in to see you?"

"Paul who?" she said.

Heather threw that right back at me in a pugnacious tone.

By treating me like just another defense attorney, she had forfeited her advantage and that was something Heather never did. I gave her a moment to cool down and regain her poise. I sat down in a faded brocade chair by the window.

"Heather, we've come a long way from the days when we used to speak frankly to each other."

"Okay, Joth."

She stood up and went to the window and stood with her back to me looking out over the Potomac.

"Do I think somebody killed Holly Sullivan?" she said. "Maybe. Do I think it was your client? If she were killed, probably yes."

She turned around abruptly.

"Sully pulled the wool over a lot of people's eyes, including yours, Joth. I never trusted him after the Duggan matter. He committed a felony and he skated."

She exhaled and took a second before continuing.

"I'm trying not to let that prejudice me. But if Sully's got nothing to hide, then get his ass in here."

"What exactly is it that you want to know?"

"I'd like to know what he knows about George Duggan."

My antennae went up.

"Duggan? What's Duggan got to do with any of this?"

"He's built a career on shady business practices, for one thing. And your client hates him."

"That's no secret."

This was so unexpected that some sixth sense told me to tread carefully. I addressed Heather with the same arm's length caution as I would any other prosecutor.

"Okay, Heather, anything more you can tell me?"

"No," she said.

That was it. This could be a dead end, at least for the day.

"There's more to it than this, isn't there?" I said.

Once again, Heather's eyes sought the safety of the window and the horizon beyond. She looked out the window, as if an answer was lurking out there somewhere.

"I don't know," she said. "Something just doesn't smell right about this."

She looked at me like she was going to say something else, but whatever it was, personal or professional, she thought better of it. As I tried to fit the pieces together, I played a hunch.

"Is there something you can tell me about George Duggan?" I said.

Heather held my eyes for a moment and then they dropped with a sigh, which left me feeling shorted.

"You know, Joth, I've got that trial I have to prepare for. Sorry."

She started straightening papers on her desk. She had said everything she was going to say, and maybe more than she originally wanted to.

"Yeah, okay," I said.

I took a moment to observe her, but she ignored me as if I'd already left the room. "Good luck on your trial, Heather."

As I got to the door, she looked up.

"Let me know if you come up with anything else, Joth, will you?"

I nodded and left, wondering what she thought I might come up with or what she thought I could even be looking to figure out. I wasn't sure myself.

Chapter Twelve

Whiskey Talks

I owned a little bungalow tucked away in a wooded section of Arlington, called Maywood, a neighborhood that had not yet been gentrified, although I waited anxiously for the day when I could sell my little house and make some money.

The living room was situated on the left side of the first floor, which is where I spent most of my time. Paul showed up unannounced on Saturday night during the second period of the Caps game I was watching on TV.

"Who's winning?" he said, without looking at the screen.

"The Redskins."

He gave me a pro forma chuckle as he started pacing back and forth, distracted, poking at books on a shelf, picking up magazines off the coffee table and examining objects on the mantlepiece. I followed his movements quizzically.

"You want a beer, Paul?"

"Whiskey if you got it."

I was surprised. It was one thing to find him drunk at his sister's funeral, but as a rule, Paul was not a drinker. He'd long ago learned he couldn't handle it.

"Let me see what I can do."

I found half empty pint in the kitchen and returned with the bottle, a can of Coke and a glass full of ice. Paul was staring out the window into my tiny backyard with his hands stuffed into the back pockets of his jeans.

"So what brings you to this part of Arlington?"

"I was just passing by."

I laughed. I didn't believe him, and he didn't expect me to. He set the glass on the mantlepiece and mixed the drink himself, going heavy on the whiskey.

"It's been a rough month, Joth," he said. "To you, this is just a case. But I lost my sister. Everybody I know is involved in this, and my life's turned upside down. Look at you. In college you were my mentor and friend, and now you're taking sides against me."

"I'm not taking sides with or against anyone, Paul. I just don't want my old friend to be prosecuted for a crime he didn't commit."

"You've got a lot of confidence in him, Joth. I know Sully a lot better than you."

"Do you?"

"Look, I don't think Sully killed my sister. I think what happened was inevitable. It's just sordid and so damn ugly. It gets to you, you know?"

I was surprised by Paul's change of tune, so I immediately probed for a reason.

"What are you really worried about? George Duggan?"

The lights in the room were turned down, so I couldn't make out his expression, but he took an impulsive step toward me and stopped.

"Why would I be worried about George Duggan?"

"From what everybody tells me, he's a dangerous man."

Paul stifled a sort of guttural laugh.

"I hardly know him, Joth. But I'll tell you who's scared of him. Sully."

"Why should Sully be scared of Duggan?"

Paul sat down and took a long sip of his drink.

"Blackmail."

"Blackmail?"

"Yes," he said.

His voice was so subdued I barely heard him.

"Sully's blackmailing Duggan?"

"If I tell you, you won't tell Sully that I told you?"

"Of course I will, he's my client. He's also my friend."

"I thought I was your friend. Look, I'm carrying some dangerous information, Joth, and I don't like it."

I remembered what Sully had said while we were shooting pool, that Holly was blackmailing Duggan.

"Why would Sully be doing that?"

"I don't know. Revenge? Duggan brought him down after all."

"Blackmail is serious business, Paul. That doesn't really seem to be Sully's style, does it?"

"Maybe not."

Paul seemed ready to let it go, but I wasn't.

"What does Sully have on Duggan that could add up to blackmail?"

Paul took another long drink.

"Are you kidding? Duggan was the dirtiest guy in the county."

"I'm listening."

"You look back at the deals that Duggan's done. Look at the variances and setback exceptions he's gotten. Look at the deals on affordable housing that never quite materialized after the building went up. This goes to the highest reaches in the county, Joth."

"And you being a rival contractor . . ."

"And a tax-paying citizen, dammit. I don't like to see it. I don't even like to know about it."

"But you're suddenly willing to squeeze your brother-in-law while Duggan gets away with this?"

"I'm not scared of my brother-in-law."

Paul seemed fidgety. He walked over to the bookcase and began moving knickknacks around like pieces on an unfamiliar game board with the same idle curiosity he had displayed when I caught him nosing around in my desk at work.

Among the objects was the Jefferson Cup Sully had given me as a groomsman's gift at his wedding. Paul knocked it over and the key that was in it fell to the floor. I picked it up and lifted it up with a show of annoyance. It was heavy and ornate like the antique pistol case it kept secure. Inside the case was a .38 Diamondback revolver that Sully had given me for Christmas one year.

"Keep your hands off it," I said.

Paul saw me glance at the pistol case as I put the key back in the cup. He had an identical cup in his own house and studied the date etched in the pewter, perhaps remembering better times.

"Joth, I don't think you should be keeping the key to a gun case in something you got at a wedding. Bad karma."

"Little late for that now, don't you think?"

I put the cup back where it had been. Paul shoved his hands in his pockets as if he didn't trust their capacity for mischief and began examining the volumes of literature, unread since college, that I had displayed on the shelves.

"It's not so much that I'm scared of Duggan. It's complicated."

"Like he's got something on you?"

I said this lightly, just trying to draw him out. Paul spun around like a top.

"What would he have on me?" he said, sounding shocked, but impatient, too.

He was getting drunk and beginning to slur his words. I knew I'd hit on something and I wondered what it was.

"You've got to keep up with the competition, Paul, don't you?"

He had left the Coke and bourbon on the mantel-piece, so he walked over and made himself another drink. When he was done, he stirred it with his finger and sat down, holding the drink in his lap.

"I haven't had a project in a couple of years. Duggan gets 'em all. And now you know why."

"Why don't you go tell Heather about this?"

"She knows. He's smart, Joth. Sully's a crafty guy and look what he did to him."

"And now Sully's getting him back."

Paul sipped his drink slowly to avoid replying.

"You think Sully would do the development deal with Duggan?" I said.

"He's not getting that property, Joth."

"You gonna be able to drive, Paul?"

"I don't know."

Paul seemed suddenly aware of his current condition.

"Can you put me up?"

I shook my head in disgust. It had been a long time since I'd had to put up a drunken Paul Saunders.

"Look, let's just watch the game, huh? I'm worn out by all this stuff and I bet you are, too."

I returned my attention to the Caps and Paul pretended to watch with me. At the end of the period, he asked what the score was.

"It's right there on the screen."

He glared at me, then returned to his favorite issue.

"If Sully would do that property swap, it would take care of a lot of issues."

"Just exactly how do you figure that would work?"

"What do you mean?"

"Are you going to qualify for the kind of construction loan you'd need?"

"Probably not. Neither would Sully."

"What gives you the advantage?"

"I know people. I could partner with someone."

"Like George Duggan?"

"If I did, it would get him off everybody's back."

"Whose back is he on besides yours?"

"He's got money, Joth. You can't subdivide and develop a parcel like that without real money."

"So you'd make a deal with the devil?"

"I already have," Paul said.

He took a moment to amend his statement.

"We all make deals with the devil, Joth. Sully certainly did."

"And he paid a big price for it."

"I know that, cocksucker."

I felt a surge of anger in Paul's remark, but he was too drunk to be responsible for his words. I let it sit and returned my attention to the game. Soon, Paul drifted into drunken self-pity.

"You know what Sully's big mistake was?" he said. "He should have gone into business with me instead of Duggan, but he didn't trust me. And look how it turned out."

It took me a moment to realize he was talking about the debacle that cost Sully his license.

"You wanted to joint venture with Sully?"

"Sure. Back then, you could get legit financing and we could have made a fortune. But there was something about Duggan and the quick payoff he promised that Sully couldn't resist. I just think he likes the scent of danger. You take Duggan out of the mix and none of this would have happened. Holly would still be alive. They'd still be married and Sully would probably be a judge by now."

I took a moment to ponder all of that.

"He's always been a stubborn man," I said. "Tell me something, Paul. That girl Lori that he's seeing. Did Sully start dating her before or after Holly died?"

"How the hell should I know?"

"I'm just curious."

"It doesn't matter. They broke up," he said. "He's dating a cop now."

"Is he?"

A vision of Officer Christine Kelleher, the high school security officer popped into my head and I wondered if it could be her.

"Yeah," Paul said. "You know Sully; he can charm anyone, but we'll see how good she is to him."

I didn't respond. I gave it a minute and leaned forward to get a better look. Paul was sound asleep. I checked my watch and roused him.

"You know where the extra bedroom is. There are towels in the linen closet. The sheets on the bed are reasonably clean."

Paul didn't look like he cared. He made his way upstairs and I watched the end of the game. In the morning
when I got up, he was gone.

Chapter Thirteen

No Sign of Violence

I met George Duggan several years earlier during Sully's difficulties. My goal at the time was to pin the real estate scam on George in an effort to save Sully's hide, but Duggan anticipated every line of attack and parried my every move like an Olympic fencer. He had prepared for the day their scheme would collapse and had planned from the start to make sure Sully took the fall.

I picked up the phone to call him, then thought better of it. Instead, I found his address online and drove over to his house on Arlington Ridge Road.

Duggan ran his real estate operation out of his home, a large, rambling Tudor, with a breathtaking view of the Potomac and the Capitol rising in a panorama from his back porch. It was early, especially to show up unannounced. I parked in the circular driveway where several days of *Washington Posts* were lying in their protective wrappers, walked up to the broad double door and rang the bell. When no one answered, I knocked. Again, nobody responded. I checked several windows. No sign of life inside.

Under the overhang of two white oaks was a two-car garage attached to the left side of the house. I strolled over and peeked through a window streaked with several months of grime. One bay was empty and the other was occupied by a Land Rover. As I watched Duggan's neighbors start up their cars and head off to work, I checked his mailbox, which was stuffed with uncollected mail.

I went back to my office to mull over the situation.

I called Paul Saunders and asked him to meet me at Whitlow's for coffee. He agreed and suggested breakfast. As I arrived, I saw he was already there.

It was late morning on a weekday and the place was empty. Paul had selected the most secluded table in the bar area, which was fine with me. He lifted a mug of black coffee and waved his arm for Johnny to come take our order.

"What'll you have?" he said.

"Hey Paul. A Coke sounds good to me," I said.

"Something to eat?" he said. "Late breakfast? Early lunch?"

I looked at him curiously.

"I think I'll pass."

When Johnny arrived, Paul wasted no time ordering a cheese omelet, bacon and an English muffin.

"Sure you won't have something?" he said. "I hate to eat alone."

I shook my head at Johnny.

"What time did you leave my house this morning?"

"I don't know," said Paul. "Early. It was still dark out."

"You have any trouble getting home?"

He sipped at his coffee as if it were still too hot.

"Oh, so you're going to be big brother again."

"I'm just worried about you, Paul."

"This is about business," he said.

He sounded as if he had scheduled our meeting.

"Is it?" I said. "What kind of business?"

"You don't understand the real estate world, my friend."

"Why don't you tell me about it?"

"It's about patience and the periodic big score. All you have to do is read the paper to know that. The face of northern Virginia is changing on a daily basis. I'll get my share. I always have. And that, Joth Proctor, is the key to prosperity."

Paul was always a moody sort of guy, but he was acting inexplicably ebullient that morning, considering his condition just twelve hours earlier. I concluded he was drunk. Not still drunk—drunk again.

"In my business," I said, "it's about having enough clients who can afford the fees. In yours, it's about owning a developable piece of real estate, isn't it?"

"That, and some financing."

The food came and Paul dug in like he hadn't eaten in a week. I took a steady look at him and waited for him to stop eating.

"Paul, if I get Sully to swap you the property, how are you going to finance the development?"

"Did you talk some sense into him? Is that why we're here?"

"He's thinking about it. But it only makes sense if you can develop it."

"Don't worry about that. I've got the contacts."

I thought back to my excursion that morning.

"George Duggan?"

"I'm sure he'd do it," Paul said, through a mouthful of eggs. "If the numbers worked."

"Have you spoken to him about it?"

"No," he said dismissing the idea. "Why would I? I haven't got the property yet."

"How well do you know George Duggan?"

Paul stopped and put his fork down.

"You know how many real estate developers there are in northern Virginia?"

"You told me he got all the deals."

171

"All the deals graft can buy, Joth."

"You didn't answer my question. How well do you know him?"

"Not well," he said. "We're in the same business. I don't know why you keep bringing him up."

"Sully owns the property."

"Sully *thinks* he does."

"Why wouldn't Duggan partner on the development with him?"

Paul laughed maliciously.

"Come on, Joth. That's not going to happen, and you know why. Sully hated him and distrusted him, and for good reason, as you know better than anyone. No telling what Sully might do to Duggan if he had the chance."

"Really? Such as what?"

"Anything's possible. Can't say I'd blame him."

"But you'd work with him. He ruined your brother-in-law and your sister, but you'd still work with him."

"I'm a businessman. If this deal goes down, it would all be forgotten. At least it would with me."

"Have you discussed it with him?"

Paul hesitated and moved his eggs around with his fork.

"In general terms, yeah. Of course that was a while ago."

"When's the last time you saw him?" I said.

"Why?"

"Just curious."

"You're never just curious, Joth. You're a goddamn busybody."

I ignored that because Paul was right.

"What did your sister have on Duggan?" I said.

That stopped Paul in his tracks. He looked around as if he was suspicious of eavesdroppers, as if he had already said too much.

"She had nothing to do with George Duggan. Ever."

"That's not what I hear, Paul."

"From who?"

"Did she, or didn't she?"

He mastered the momentary flare of temper and pushed his plate away.

"Well Holly's dead, so it doesn't matter, does it? And that leaves Sully and Duggan. And that's complicated, Joth. They hated each other, Sully and Duggan. But there was stuff going on between them through a back channel."

I leaned in a little to hear more.

"You know Sully. He's always got something going. Duggan's the same way."

"I didn't know you knew that much about Duggan."

Paul shifted uncomfortably in his seat.

"Sully and Duggan, they each saw a way to play the other. Rumors got started because Holly was in the middle. But let me tell you something about my sister. People tried to keep her in the dark, but she paid attention."

I wanted to ask him what he meant by that, but I had a pretty good idea. Her brother and her husband had been leveraging whatever she knew for their best interest, probably while trying to convince the poor woman that her best interest was aligned with theirs.

"So this deal, if Sully controlled it, was a way to stick it to Duggan and even the score?"

Paul had finished his breakfast. He wiped his mouth with his napkin and threw it on the plate.

"I don't know. Probably. Sully wants the property, but he'd never pass on a chance to get even with Duggan. Make no mistake about that. You can bet on it. Go ask him. He'll tell you himself."

Paul got up, took thirty dollars out of his wallet and put it on the table.

"Don't worry," I said. "He's next on the list."

But he wasn't. I sat at the corner table a little longer, nursing a second Coke. As the lunch crowd drifted in, I ordered the special without checking to see what it was. I ate it without any appetite, taking my time as I chewed

over my conversation with Paul. No matter how I reassembled the situation, it all led to the same place.

I paid my bill and walked down Wilson Boulevard to her office.

Betty told me she was at lunch. At first, I didn't believe her and became so insistent that she pointed out the Rotary speech inscribed on her daily calendar. I calmed down and told her I'd wait.

"She has a hearing at two."

"I've got all day."

I was never pushy with Betty and she knew it meant something when I was. Heather must have come in the back way because I didn't see her, but at 1:45 on the dot Betty led me into her office. I didn't sit down and neither did Heather.

"I'd like to know more about George Duggan," I said.

"What would I know about George Duggan?"

I decided to lay my cards on the table.

"I'm wondering if anyone has reported him missing."

Heather seemed to consider her answer carefully.

"Who would do that? He lives and works alone. He doesn't have any family."

It took me a moment to process her answer.

"You know a lot about him."

"How much do you know, Joth?"

"I know there's a bunch of newspapers sitting in his driveway."

"Maybe he's on vacation."

"Duggan's too careful a guy to forget to cancel his paper. Or his mail."

"You're probably right."

"So?"

Heather sat down at her desk. I watched a fan of wrinkles etch themselves between her eyebrows as she thought for a moment. A few seconds later, she leaned forward decisively and folded her hands.

"His car was found near Potomac Yards four days ago. It was locked and no one was in it."

It took me a moment to digest this news.

"Did he have property there?"

She considered her answer, but it was public record.

"Yes. A commercial property, not far from the Parkway. One of his employees called when Duggan missed an appointment and didn't answer his phone."

"Any sign of him?"

"No."

"Any sign of violence?"

"No."

I took a deep breath and tried to think it through.

"He was known to carry a lot of money in his wallet."

This was a wild shot and Heather knew it, so she refused to rise to the bait.

"There are some things I can't tell you, Joth."

Few people who knew Heather Burke could read her moods and expressions as well as I could, and she was making no effort to hide any of it. She knew me just as well and waited for me to speak.

"Your investigation and the questions you were asking yesterday," I said, "have me thinking that this is no longer about Holly Saunders, is it? It's about Duggan."

"Maybe."

"Paul's been in here telling tall tales about what Sully might be willing to do to Duggan and that's why you want to talk to my client."

Heather stared at me and didn't flinch, which told me all I'd come to find out.

"I guess you have a hearing at two," I said.

"I guess I do."

I got up and started for the door.

"Joth," she said, in a considerate tone that made me pause. "Be careful, will you?"

I nodded.

"Thanks, Heather. I will."

Chapter Fourteen

In the Water, In the Hole

I couldn't reach Sully on his cell phone, so I called Kevin Riley, the only person I knew who had a hand in every element of the local real estate market.

"Hey, Riley, it's Joth Proctor."

"If you're calling about Sully's rent, he's still behind and he hasn't moved out. And if that's not why you're calling, please tell him I asked you about it."

"Actually, I'm calling about somebody else. Paul Saunders."

"Paul Saunders?"

He repeated the name with an edge of distaste.

"You see much of him?" I said.

"Used to. He had a commercial property I managed, but he sold it."

I floated a long shot.

"I guess he's going to get you involved in the new project when it goes up?"

"The one he's doing with Duggan?" Riley said. "Did he tell you that?"

"Paul says he needs a top realtor and you're a guy he's used before."

"I hope so. But that's like the lost Beach Boys' album. You hear a lot about it, but it's just a lot of smoke as far as I can tell."

"Who do you hear about it from?" I said. "Duggan or Paul?"

Riley laughed.

"Duggan and Paul are polar opposites, you know. Duggan's cards are always close to his vest, but Paul—he doesn't wear any underwear."

"Look, Paul's okay, but he's dumb as a post. Duggan's ruthless and I'm a little worried he might try to cut Paul out."

"I don't see how," said Riley. "It's Paul's property. Besides, all Duggan cares about is if the numbers work."

"Have you seen the property?"

"Nope. I don't even know where it is. There'll be plenty of time for that if they ever break ground."

"I suppose you're right," I said. "You know anything about the deal?"

"No, I don't know the details, Joth, just that Paul's talked to me about marketing it for them."

"How close is it to getting off the ground, as far as you know?"

"You know Paul. To hear him talk, they're always two weeks away from breaking ground."

"Thanks for the information, Riley. By the way, what's the name of Paul's LLC?"

He thought about it for a minute.

"Belle Terra Properties. Something like that. Belle is the first word in the name."

After I hung up, I walked over to the courthouse to search through the county land records. Paul owned his home and the undevelopable single-family property he'd tried to trade to Sully. Other than that, neither he nor his LLC owned any property in the county.

It had been a long day and I was exhausted. I went to bed to sleep on the information I'd gathered over the last few days. But something felt dreadfully wrong. Slipping in and out of consciousness throughout the night, I was haunted by faces I used to know. They bobbed up in front of me like marionettes in a children's puppet show, swapping tokens of love and friendship and betrayal, their strings barely visible in the half-light of the stage show. I knew I couldn't trust appearances and had to probe deeper.

Around four in the morning, I gave up. I threw on a bathrobe, went downstairs and made a pot of coffee. Outside, the stars were bright in a moonless sky, and the balmy air proclaimed a crisp spring morning was on the horizon.

There was more to this than Paul and Sully spatting over a piece of real estate, like schoolboys fighting over the prom queen. They were among the most stubborn and competitive men I had ever known, and each would be happy to get one over on the other. They both needed the property as a financial lifeline and each of them seemed desperate to control it. Neither could develop it without a partner with money or know-how, but none of that explained the premium they placed on a single piece of real property.

That's what kept bringing me back to the face that had stared at me through the night: George Duggan, who hadn't been seen in days and whose empty car had been found in South Arlington.

Duggan was missing and Tom Sullivan had reason to hate him, but there was something else I couldn't put my finger on. I took a shower and pulled on a sweatshirt and jeans. Then I checked the glove box of my car and tested the batteries of a flashlight I kept there.

It had been several years since I had done any in-the-field detective work, but I didn't lose that much sleep for nothing, and I was determined to find out what my gut was telling me.

The rising sun was just tingeing the eastern sky with pink as I drove north on Glebe Road. I turned off on a gravel road that connected the house where Holly died to the rest of the world. It was less of a neighborhood than a collection of widely separated, mismatched houses, built on cleared patches of wooded land.

I drove past the Saunders family property, parked fifty yards down the street and took the flashlight from the glove box. It was quiet, except for a few dogs barking and the sound of robins and cardinals waking up. Someone drove down the street tossing papers in driveways. I waited for him to pass.

The white brick house was situated on the front of the lot, squarely facing the road. Behind it, a yard of brown grass stretched away into the evergreens and budding hardwoods. There were no cars in the driveway or on the street in front of the house. I walked cautiously up to the concrete stoop and tried the front door. It was locked, as I assumed it would be. There were no lights visible inside. Working my way around to the back, I checked the kitchen door, which was also locked.

I didn't know what I was looking for—a broken window, scrap of paper, something left by a careless intruder—or inspiration, perhaps.

From the road, a blacktop driveway led up to a detached wood-frame garage. Up to a line parallel with the front of it, the grass had the appearance of an untended lawn, waiting to be refreshed by warm weather. Beyond it, the weeds were ankle deep, like a vacant lot.

Standing at the top of the driveway as the rising sun gave clarity to the day, I made out a faint track through the morning mist and underbrush, as if someone had trampled it down by repeated visits into the yard. Panning my flashlight, I followed the track. It led toward a copse of dogwoods marking the beginning of adjacent woods. Ten feet short of the trees, a rough circle of about eight feet in circumference had been disturbed by recent digging. It enclosed a low mound of churned earth roughly covered by the stalks of tall grass that had once stood there.

I kicked at the dirt, which was loose. An overpowering sensation of dread came over me. I fought it back, refusing to assume anything or to name the awful possibilities that occurred to me in that brief moment of insight.

I followed the path back to the garage. I knew that Sully typically kept keys under the mat on the stoop, but all that remained of the mat was a grimy silhouette, marking where it had recently been. I soon found the key on the ledge above the doorframe, not in its usual place.

Inside, among the yard tools, I found a garden spade. I carried it back to the mound at the back of the yard. I pushed the toe of the spade into the earth and slowly, cautiously, started digging. The loose earth moved easily.

There was a chill in the morning air, but I was perspiring freely before I'd removed a foot of the loose Virginia clay. As I dug the toe of the spade in again, it butted up against something that could have been a tree root but probably wasn't. I tapped at it, scrapped the earth away and shined my flashlight into the hole. I scraped away some more dirt and shrunk backwards when what I was looking at took shape.

It was a heavy work boot. There was a foot in the boot and a leg attached to the foot. I steadied myself against the spade, then stumbled the short distance into the shelter of the dogwoods and collapsed against a tree trunk. I sat there and re-gathered myself. I knew I needed to call the police, but first I had to figure out what they would ask me, what I would say, and what my obligations were to my client, if I still had one.

I also knew I had to find out who was in that hole.

I was still there five minutes later when my phone rang. It was Heather.

"You know where Rock Spring Park is?" she said.

After a moment's consideration, I answered her.

"Isn't that the little pocket park between the two sections of North George Mason Drive?"

"That's right. How long will it take you to get here?"

There was something in the tone of her voice I didn't like. I glanced at the pile of disturbed dirt and decided to save that news. I felt numb, too numb to argue with her.

"Ten minutes?" I said.

"Be here in five."

In a leafy, residential area a half-mile from the Fairfax County line, two sections of North George Mason Drive are separated by a three-hundred-yard run of well-kept woods, fringing both banks of a meandering creek called Rock Spring. The stream that disappears beneath the street at both ends of the park bisects a neighborhood of single-family homes. A bike path runs the length of the park, paralleling the stream and joining the two disconnected sections of George Mason. At the south end, where I pulled up and parked, yellow police tape blocked access to the bike path and the park.

A knot of fifteen or twenty curious citizens had gathered in the mist. I saw early morning walkers, joggers and birdwatchers, all angling and stretching for a view of what lay beyond in the narrow, wooded park.

I gave my name to the officer stationed there. He checked my ID, looked me over quickly and called to another officer, who escorted me back.

An ambulance had pulled up on the grass at the far end of the park and med techs and police officers were loading something into it—something covered by a sheet. I shuddered.

When Heather saw me, she ordered them to stop. She was wearing a wool sweater and jeans, an outfit that told me how suddenly she'd left her house. My knees were muddy, and I was in a full sweat, which she must have noticed.

"Are you going to tell me, or do you want me to guess?" I said.

With a gesture of her head, she led me back up the bike path to the ambulance. She stopped when we got there and looked down at the shape under the sheet. I knew who it was when I noticed the waterlogged shoe with the missing tassel.

"This isn't going to be easy for you, Joth."

"I know."

As she pulled back a corner of the sheet, I could feel her watching my expression. It was Sully, his hair and clothing soaking wet. He was dressed in business clothes, and his once-handsome face—now white and bloated—still bore the remnant of the bruise Paul had given him.

I thought about the body in the hole and blew out my breath in a long whistle. "What happened?" I said, though it was apparent he had drowned.

She looked me over again.

"I was hoping you could help us with that."

It was my turn to measure her expression, probing and suspicious, and I felt my stomach churn. I took Sully's cold, lifeless hand. Vignettes that had been buried for years flashed through my mind, good days of laughter and unlimited promise.

"Sorry," I said. "Don't think I can."

"When's the last time you talked to him?"

"You're used to this, Heather. I'm not."

"Do you want to sit down?"

"I haven't seen him in four or five days. Maybe more."

"You didn't meet him here last night?"

My head swiveled toward her.

"No."

She snapped her fingers and a uniformed officer appeared, bearing a Ziplock evidence bag. She took a cell phone out of the bag and pushed the power button.

"Recognize this?"

"They all look alike, Heather. Is there some point to all this?"

The phone powered up with a beep and she accessed a program.

"How did you get the security code?"

"It was easy. Dave."

"So it's Sully's?"

"Was."

"Has anybody told Sully's kids?"

"Not yet," she said.

Heather was a tough professional with a job to do, but I saw the red around her eyes. This marked the end of a segment of her life, too. She pulled up the calendar function on the phone and showed it to me.

On the eleven o'clock line of the previous night it read: "Meeting with J-P."

It didn't give a reason or a place, just a note in a line in his calendar. I stared at it and waited for the inevitable question.

"J-P," she said. "Isn't that you?"

"I didn't have an appointment with Sully, and I didn't see him last night."

"I don't suppose you were here last night at eleven o'clock?"

"Nope."

I shook my head, feeling numb.

"How do you explain this, Joth?"

"I don't. Now, I have something you need to hear."

"More important than this?"

"There's something I need to show you."

"What are you talking about?"

"Not too far from here."

"Related to this?"

I sucked in my breath.

"I don't know."

Heather looked at me with intense curiosity and waited for more.

"How many homicide detectives do you have here?"

She glanced up as if to affirm her recollection.

"Kearney and his deputy."

"Well, leave one of them here to finish up. Bring the other one, and an officer, and come with me."

It was a unique request for an unprecedented situation. It took Heather several seconds to make up her mind, but her work here was done. She called out to Kearney and the second officer and gave them the orders.

"We'll take Kearney's car," she said.

I gave directions. Like estranged lovers, we settled into opposite corners of the backseat, each mulling our own issues and concerns until the squad car pulled up in front of the Saunders property.

The sun was up by then, and the bright morning light illuminated the chipped brick and faded trim of the little rambler. I led them up the blacktop driveway. Long years of legal training told me to remain silent, but my story spilled out through an unedited stream of consciousness.

"I couldn't sleep. Everything I thought about kept running back to this property. So I came here this morning, just to poke around and see what struck me."

At the top of the driveway, I pointed out the trail through the tall grass.

"Then I noticed this."

I led them single file through the weeds and ground fog until we reached the mound of dirt beside the partially empty hole.

"I followed the track back to here. When I saw it, I started digging."

Heather and Kearney exchanged glances. Kearney got down on all fours with his face in the pit.

"Where'd you get the shovel?" Heather said.

"In the garage."

"Was it open?"

"No."

"How'd you get in?"

"I found the key. Jesus, Heather!"

Kearney was a tall, squarely built man and he straightened up with an effort.

"There's something there," he said to Heather, but she had already noticed the dirt-encrusted boot.

"What do you know about that?"

"Only what you see."

Kearney had a camera with him. He snapped a series of photographs and backed away when he was done, looking to Heather for instructions. The uniformed officer's nameplate read Butler. He picked up the spade and looked at Heather. She nodded.

Butler dug like an archeologist, using the blade of the spade to push the dirt to the side and slowly the form of the body began to take shape.

"Heather, I'm not used to this sort of thing," I said.

I reached for her arm. She patted my hand once consolingly, then firmly removed it from her elbow.

"You don't have to watch if you don't want to," she said.

"My car's back at the park."

"Don't you want to know who it is?"

"I know who it is," I said. So do you. It's Paul Saunders."

She called Kearney's name and told him to drive me back to the park.

"Do you know the Starbucks at Lyon Village Shopping Center?" she said.

I nodded dully.

"Meet me there in an hour."

No one said a word on the short drive back to my car. I drove home and took my second shower of the day, trying to wash off the sweat and grime and the sordid feeling that surrounds not just death, but lives gone wrong—ended just like that by someone else's desperation.

Chapter Fifteen

Bitter Coffee

It was a little before nine when I got to Starbucks. Most of the morning commuter crowd had departed. I ordered black coffee and huddled over the steaming cup at a corner table, taking stock of what just happened.

Heather arrived twenty minutes late. She stopped at the bar and ordered coffee and I waited for her to join me. She looked like hell and I knew I did, too. I reminded myself to be more circumspect when talking to the chief prosecutor about a pair of deaths.

"Who was it?" I said.

"Who do you think?"

"I told you what I think."

"We won't know for a couple of days, Joth; not 'til the forensics come in."

"It was Paul, wasn't it?"

"I can't tell you."

I sipped my coffee and tried to read her face. I wasn't ready to move on to the obvious follow-up—who might have done it.

"How'd you happen to be there, Joth?"

"It keeps coming back to that, doesn't it? That property?"

"What did you think you were going to find?"

"I don't know, Heather. Something . . . something that would help me put the pieces together."

"Where were you last night?" she said.

"When?"

"All night."

"Home."

"Alone?"

"Unfortunately."

That little back-and-forth sat for a minute as we sipped our coffee.

"Was Sully paying you?"

"What are you talking about?"

"I don't see you around the courthouse much anymore. Business a little slow?"

"It's all right. Am I under arrest?"

"You know you're not."

"Then I can leave?"

"Of course."

I stayed where I was.

"Joth, I've got to ask these questions."

"No, you don't."

"You'll be getting them again from a detective."

"I hope he'll be more polite."

"I've got to run everything down, Joth. Especially you. I have to be impartial."

I shrugged a shoulder to acknowledge this truth.

"Do we know when he died?" I said. "Or how?"

"Which one? Sully or the guy in the hole?"

"Sully. He was my friend. Yours, too."

She ignored this. I knew Heather wouldn't let sentiment get in the way.

"Nothing's official," she said. "I've ordered an inquest and an autopsy. We'll know more in a few days, but I think it's safe to say he drowned."

She gave me a few moments to think.

"I know this is a lot to digest, Joth. But I want to know what you know."

"I don't know anything about it, Heather."

Her face was grim.

"When's the last time you saw Paul Saunders?"

I assumed Paul was in the hole, so this was the dangerous ground I had worried about. I knew Heather wouldn't back off, so I jumped in.

"I had lunch with him day before yesterday. Breakfast, actually."

"Where?"

"Whitlow's."

"What did you talk about?"

"I wanted to know what happened to Holly."

"Why?"

"Why?"

The question offended me. I knew that showed on my face, but I was willing to let her see it.

"Yes, why. You say Sully's your client. He's not being charged with anything. Certainly he didn't hire you to find out what happened to his wife."

For the first time I realized how dull I'd grown and how dull I must have sounded. I had no professional interest in Holly's death, at least not yet.

"Because I cared about her, Heather. Because I cared about them all."

This was true, but I didn't know if it would satisfy her. I had no other explanation, though, until I thought of another way to ask the question I wanted answered.

"Where was Paul last night?" I said.

"I heard he was in D.C."

"D.C.?" I said. "What was he doing there?"

"There's reason to believe he spent the night at a hotel in Southeast," she said.

That didn't sound right. She watched me to gauge my reaction.

" 'Evidence to believe?' I get the sense you don't, Heather. Does it check out?"

She looked at her watch. Conversations like this usually have a limited shelf life.

196

"I don't know," she said. "He was due in my office five minutes ago."

"If he's still alive," I said.

She stood up.

"The police will be by to see you. After they do, give me a call, Joth. I'll want to talk to you."

"Do I need to bring a lawyer?"

She smiled, the first one I'd seen all day.

"Joth, I don't think you killed your best friend."

After she left, I sat for a minute. It was a long time since I'd thought of Sully as my best friend, but even after all these years, there was no second candidate.

Two police officers showed up at my office that afternoon. Lamprey was a plainclothes detective. He showed me his badge. I recognized his partner.

"Hello Officer Kelleher. I thought you were assigned to the high school."

"Assignments change," she said.

She didn't even crack half a smile. I looked at Lamprey and wondered if he knew his partner had investigated the Brownie Bust. He began by politely apologizing for not calling ahead.

"We're right around the corner," he said. "It's easier just to walk over."

And much easier to investigate when your subject hasn't had a chance to prepare.

I nodded.

Lamprey was a tall, heavyset man with carefully cultivated black hair that he wore moussed and combed to one side. His hands told me he was married and left-handed. I took an immediate dislike to him.

Kelleher's job was to take notes, which she did on an iPad after asking my permission and reading me my rights.

"I suppose you know why we're here?" Lamprey said.

I decided not to waste time on the usual semantic dance.

"I assume you are here about what happened this morning."

"I know Mr. Sullivan was a friend of yours," he said, "and I'm sorry. Anything you can tell us to help us catch his killer?"

"So he was murdered?"

"We're treating it as a murder, yes."

"How did he die?"

The two officers shared disgruntled looks for my benefit. I didn't bother to show my appreciation because I was already annoyed to have them in my office.

"We'll get to that," said Lamprey. "I understand you had an appointment with him last night?"

I shook my head.

"That's not true."

"Your name was in his calendar," Kelleher said.

She looked sharply at me, as if she'd caught me red-handed.

" 'Eleven p.m. meeting with J-P.' "

I took a careful look at her, and as I did, I recalled what Paul had told me, that Sully had been dating a cop.

"J-P is not my name and I don't meet anybody at eleven o'clock."

Lamprey resumed the inquiry.

"Do you know where you were?"

"Yes, I do."

"Any witnesses?"

"I live alone."

He nodded sorrowfully, as if he'd heard that one before, which I'm sure he had, but he persisted. Kelleher seemed especially interested in hearing my answer.

"Any witnesses?"

"No."

"When did you last see Mr. Sullivan?" she said.

I was careful to tell them the same thing I told Heather.

"I've been trying to figure that out. Four or five days ago."

"Where was that?"

"I dropped by his house."

"Any particular reason?"

"We're friends. Old friends. Just social."

"Anybody else there?"

"No."

"What did you talk about?"

"Things old buddies talk about. Sports, girlfriends . . . stuff like that."

I looked at Kelleher as I let my answer drift away.

"You represented him, did you not?"

I looked back at Lamprey.

"On some things, yes."

"Did you have any attorney–client discussions?"

I smiled and told him I hadn't. That meant that I couldn't duck behind privilege, but it also told the two of them that I didn't feel the need to guard against a prejudicial disclosure.

Lamprey knew that with Sully dead and no other witnesses, I could say whatever I wanted. Since he couldn't disprove anything, I remained on safe ground. All he could do was ask perfunctory questions.

"Did Mr. Sullivan mention his late wife the last time you saw him?"

"I don't think so."

"Did you think that was odd, with her death being so recent?"

"There was nothing about the conversation I considered odd. Sully was trying to move through a bad part of his life."

"Did he seem nervous, anxious, angry?"

"No, nothing out of the ordinary. He was a placid guy and that's the way he came across that night."

As I heard myself answer, it started to sink in. That was the last time I would ever see him.

"What about this dispute with his brother-in-law, Mr. Paul Saunders?"

This was the part that I wanted to hear.

"Who was in the hole?" I said.

"We don't know who was in the hole, Mr. Proctor."

"I'll bet you've got a pretty good idea."

Lamprey ignored the question and Kelleher had nothing to add.

"When's the last time you talked to Mr. Saunders?" he said.

"Two days ago. We had breakfast at Whitlow's."

"Just the two of you?" she said.

"Just the two of us. He'll tell you that, if he's still alive. Maybe you've already asked him. I don't know."

Lamprey nodded, acknowledging my play for information.

"Mr. Proctor, you know I can't get into that."

"Why not?"

I allowed myself to get excited because I wanted that to get back to Heather. As if I was disappointed in my mild insubordination, I clamped my mouth shut and ran my hand through my hair.

"Did you talk about Mr. Sullivan?"

I looked from one cop to the other and didn't answer. Then I stood up.

"Look, I appreciate you coming by, but I've got a client coming in."

"We're not quite done, Mr. Proctor."

"I am. Next time, please make an appointment."

I got a surly look from Kelleher, but they left. I gave them time to exit the building and watched them cross the parking lot. Neither of them spoke a word to the other, just another day on the beat in Arlington. I called Heather. She said she could fit me in at three o'clock. Then I called Paul at each of his numbers. No answer at any of them.

At three o'clock precisely, Heather shut the door to her office and sat down. Once again, she was the poised, professionally dressed, and self-assured prosecutor and we spoke with a mixture of familiarity and mistrust, like friendly poker players, or lawyers trying to work out a plea agreement.

"The police talk to you yet?" she said.

"Yeah, Lamprey and Kelleher. You know them?"

"Of course I know them."

"Did you know Kelleher was dating Sully?"

"What are you talking about?"

Paul hadn't mentioned the name of the cop, or exactly what Sully had said, but who else could it be?

"That's what I heard."

"That's what you heard? From who?"

"Heather, is this where we start putting our cards on the table?"

She cared about what I knew, but she was too smart to make a commitment until she checked it out from her end. That was fine with me.

"Let's talk about your breakfast with Paul."

"It was pretty boring to tell you the truth. And he has terrible table manners."

"What did you talk about?"

That was easy to ignore.

"After I left you, I called Paul on his cell," I said. "Then I called him on his office phone, and I called him at home. No answer anywhere."

I shifted my posture for effect.

"I want to know who was in the hole."

She gave me a disgusted look.

"It wasn't Paul. He was in here for an hour this morning. He's got an alibi for last night, like I said."

"What kind of alibi?"

It wasn't clear whose side Heather was on, or even what the sides were anymore. She knew that our relationship would give her an edge in this investigation because I'd tell her things that I wouldn't tell a cop. She wanted what I knew, but she knew she'd have to cooperate to get it.

"You know a guy named Carl Hamilton?" she said.

"Never heard of him."

"Paul took him to the Nationals game last night."

"The Nationals game?"

She watched me for a moment, then continued.

"He's a banker, Joth. Does a lot of real estate deals. Straight arrow. Serves on the vestry of his church and all that."

"How well did Paul know him?" I said.

"Don't know yet, but it all checks out. I've seen his ticket stub, and Paul's, too."

"How convenient," I said. "An unimpeachable witness."

"Yeah, I thought of that, but it is what it is. Paul checked into the Marriott Courtyard in Southeast around 5:30. He knew he was going to be drinking and he didn't want to drive back. Hard to argue with that thinking. The Courtyard is a couple of blocks from Nationals Park. After the game, he said good-bye to Hamilton and walked back to the hotel. He was there having breakfast this morning when I called him."

"Anybody see him last night?"

"The concierge at the hotel. He remembers because Paul parked in a reserved spot in the garage. He told him that would be okay, as long as he was out before eight in the morning."

"Anybody see him at breakfast?" I said.

"Not so far."

"What did the security cameras in the garage show?"

"Nothing. They weren't operational."

A light bulb went off.

"Did Paul know that?" I said.

"I don't think so. It never came up."

I took a moment to look out the window.

"Heather, who was in the hole?"

I turned and watched her consider her answer.

"Nothing official yet, Joth, but it might be George Duggan. I'm not completely sure. The body's pretty decomposed."

"Duggan," I said.

He had seemed untouchable, immune from the day-to-day infighting of a couple of small-time businesspeople. Even when I found his house empty, it didn't seem possible someone could have gotten to him.

I took a deep breath.

"I didn't expect that."

"I didn't say for sure, Joth. I was hoping you could help me."

"You think Sully killed Duggan, buried the body and drowned himself in a fit of remorse?"

"The first part might be right. And Duggan had scary friends."

"Like Jimmie Flambeau?"

"You said it. I didn't."

"You know where Jimmie Flambeau was last night?" I said.

"Yeah. He was at Riding Time, sticking dollar bills in G-strings."

"Dan Crowley tell you that?"

"Yup," she said.

"What a surprise. What do you know about Jimmie Flambeau?"

She pushed back from her desk and crossed her arms.

"I know he's from Richmond, where he was born Michael James Dragas. He started young, making book for the college crowd in Blacksburg. People started calling him the Dragon and pretty soon he outgrew that little town. So he moved to Arlington, changed his name and he really caught on."

She flew through that description with a spark of grudging admiration.

"I'm sure there are ten people ready to testify that they saw him at Riding Time last night."

"Upstanding citizens all," I said.

"It doesn't matter, Joth, because if Flambeau is behind what happened to Sully, he wouldn't have dirtied his own hands."

"Wouldn't there be some kind of record?"

"Come on, Joth, Flambeau runs a cash business."

"Couldn't you . . ."

"Shake him down?"

She laughed in a quick burst.

"Jimmie Flambeau wrote the book."

"You think the person who killed Sully made that phony appointment with me?"

She bit at a fingernail.

"Probably."

I shook my head.

"But whatever way you cut it, your theory still depends on Sully killing Duggan and I don't believe that."

Heather turned her palms up and shrugged.

"Sully owned the property and he wanted to develop it. Let's face it: hate him or not, Duggan had the kind of money and the kind of friends Sully needed."

She rolled her eyes as the possibilities played out in her mind.

"Maybe he just demanded a bigger piece of the deal than Sully was ready to give him. But we know Sully had a motive. Duggan cost him his license to practice law. Many men have killed for less."

I turned all of that over in my mind.

"So he lured him there?"

"No. I assume Duggan wanted to talk to him about the property. How he'd develop it, how they'd both get rich, that sort of crap. They had an argument, and then all of Sully's pent up rage came out and he killed him."

"With what?" I said.

"Don't know yet. From the condition of the body, I'd say it was a heavy blunt instrument. Sully—or whoever did it—struck him from behind and more than once."

"Then what?" I said.

"What does he do? He's desperate. He's got a dead body on his hands. He drags the body to a back corner of the lot, and he buries it."

"And the car?"

"And the car."

She nodded her head at this inconvenient fact.

"It seems a little beyond Sully's skill set to dispose of Duggan's car, doesn't it?"

I agreed.

"You think that's why Sully was so anxious to hang on to the property?" I said.

"Could be."

"So who killed Sully?"

Heather began rocking in her chair.

"Duggan had scary friends, Joth."

"That assumes they knew he was dead."

"It's amazing what those people seem to know."

That was all I was going to get, but it was enough for one day. I looked at my watch and told Heather I had to go. She didn't resist and I left, my head spinning with images of those last minutes of Sully's life.

Chapter Sixteen

The Friends of Jimmie Flambeau

Official word wasn't out yet, but if something happened in Arlington on the dark side of the law, Dan Crowley knew about it.

I picked the mid-afternoon lull to drop by Riding Time. Dan was behind the bar, chatting with two of his girls, perched on barstools in sheer negligees. One of them was Jade, the green-eyed girl with the great smile. I sat beside her. She paid me a cursory glance and looked to Dan for her cue. He gave her the kind of nod a parent gives to his child when the adult guests arrive. Both girls got up and disappeared.

"You've got a troubled look on your face today, counselor."

I scratched the inside of my ear as Dan slid me a cheap draft.

"You heard about what happened to Sully," I said.

"I didn't know the man."

I looked up from my drink, confused.

"I knew George Duggan, though. Liked the man. Everybody did."

It hadn't taken long for that information to find its way to Dan.

"A friend of mine is dead," I said.

He leaned across the bar on his folded forearms.

"A friend of Jimmie's is dead."

Dan's face clouded. It was the first time I'd seen anxiety etched across his features. Even Dan was afraid of Jimmie Flambeau.

"I hope Jimmie Flambeau doesn't think . . ."

"I wouldn't know what Jimmie thinks. Why don't you ask him?"

The cold edge in Dan's response concerned me. I quickly grasped for an innocuous response.

"I don't know the guy."

"I could set something up."

I shook my head. The thought unnerved me, as Dan intended.

"It's a small county we live in, Joth. Smallest in the country. Not a good place to make an enemy."

With a quick, practiced gesture, he scooped up my full glass of beer and poured it out in the sink. I watched his face, not sure what to make of it.

"Joth, we've been friends for a while, so let me give you a piece of advice. Any friend of Thomas Sullivan would be wise to steer clear of Jimmie Flambeau."

I nodded.

"No charge for the beer."

Riley finally had his property back. As their closest surviving relatives, Paul and his wife took custody of Dave and Sarah Sullivan and moved them into their oversized neocolonial home on a small lot off Ridge Road. Though I dreaded the prospect, I needed to pay them a visit.

After giving them a few days to settle in, I drove over one afternoon. On the way, I passed George Duggan's house. The newspapers had been collected from the driveway. I wondered who'd canceled the subscription.

I knocked on the door and Paul's wife answered. A woman I'd known slightly as an undergrad at UVA, Mary Saunders was a friendly, decent woman with a sunny disposition who saw only the best in everyone. This had to be the only explanation for her lengthy and apparently happy marriage to Paul Saunders.

She gave me a formal hug, but held it a beat longer than usual, her fingers closing on my arms. When she backed away, her eyes were tearing.

"It's been a tough spring."

I nodded.

"Those poor children," she said.

I nodded again, unable to find any words of comfort.

"Come in, Joth. Can I get you a cup of tea? Glass of water?"

"Water would be good, thanks."

I took a seat at the kitchen table. She opened a bottle of spring water and poured it into an ice-filled glass.

"Paul's working on a deal in D.C.," she said. "I don't know when he'll be back."

"Really. In Washington?"

"Yes. I understand he's got a line of a developable property. It must be a good one because he's over there all the time."

Mary had gained weight over the years, as we all had. She carried hers disproportionally in her hips and thighs, but she was still a pretty woman with clean features and a tawny complexion under graying hair that she wore short and wavy.

"I just pictured you in college," I said. "You were an English major, right?"

"Sure," she said, smiling. "That's how we met, Joth"

I was glad to find a comfortable topic.

"Professor Milton's modern literature class," she said. "That was spring semester of my first year."

I chuckled in appreciation at the faded memory.

"Milton. He dressed like Mark Twain."

"Looked like him, too. I thought I was in over my head in that class. You were really good to me, taking the time to help me see what he was getting at, and what was important in those great novels."

"I guess that's true, isn't it?"

"You sure knew your way around a good book," she said.

I sipped my water as more memories came back like dimly recollected scenes: a couple of cute first-year girls flirting with older boys, trading smiles for plot summaries so they wouldn't have to read the books. Mary had gone to college for her MRS degree and hadn't looked back, but I bet she still couldn't name the skipper of the *Pequod*.

"Those were good days, Joth," she said, stirring me out of my nostalgia tour.

I nodded and offered her a smile.

"Actually, Mary, I came to see Dave and Sarah. If they're around."

"Dave's upstairs. Sarah's out. Sarah's always out. Dave never is, even though he's got his dad's car."

She shrugged.

"A lot of deep water with him," I said.

"He's taken it hard, Joth, but he's come to grips with it, I guess. He'll work through it. Sarah's younger. She keeps it all bottled up. She'll wake up one day and acknowledge what happened and cry for a week."

It might be more complicated than that, I thought.

"How 'bout you guys?"

"Oh my God, we love those kids, always have. We've got plenty of room now, with our own kids gone. And this has always been more house than we need. Plenty of space. We'll treat them like our own."

"Paul has always been a guy with big plans," I said.

"Grandiose plans," she said.

She gave me a knowing nod, as if we shared a little-known secret. And perhaps we did. Paul was always a striver, always image conscious. It was natural for him to marry the cute, wholesome girl with the UVA credentials. That was all he wanted.

"Shall I go up?" I said.

I pointed toward the formal staircase in the foyer.

"Let me call up to him."

Mary went upstairs. A few minutes later, Dave came down. I met him at the bottom of the stairs, where he shook my hand.

"Thanks for coming by," he said.

I couldn't help noticing how grave he sounded.

"Dave, I can't tell you how sorry I am. You know, your dad meant a great deal to me. I don't even know where to begin."

"Thank you."

"This is so difficult," I said. "I'm sorry, Dave."

"I know. I know."

215

"Hard to know what to say."

"Yeah."

After a few minutes of this back and forth, I was already angling for an exit, but Dave was ready to talk.

"Do you have a minute or two?" he said.

"Of course."

He showed me into the library and shut the door. Like much of the living space of the house, the library was both elegant and sterile, as if no living person ever entered the room, let alone used it. Mahogany bookshelves were filled with mass-produced classics in faux-leather bindings and arcane sets that appeared to have been purchased at estate sales, then shelved and never read. The furnishings were uniformly Pottery Barn and displayed just like they were in the catalogue.

I took a seat on a leather couch and Dave sat across from me in a swivel chair in front of the desk. I expressed my condolences again, but he turned the subject quickly.

"There's talk I'm hearing that my dad was involved with what happened to Mr. Duggan," he said.

He spoke unemotionally and looked me squarely in the eye, but his jaw ground with tension. Dave's torment generated a sympathetic anger in me, and I probably let it show. He wanted the truth and he deserved it.

"What kind of talk?" I said. "Who's saying that?"

"Kids are saying it at school."

"Kids'll say anything, Dave, come on."

"They get it from somewhere."

I had to give him a nod on that one.

"Your dad was the finest guy I knew. And he wouldn't be involved in anything like that. He just wouldn't."

A wry smile crossed his face.

"Thanks, Mr. Proctor. I know the first part's not true. Nice try. But I care about the second part."

He had the deep-set gray-blue eyes, just like his father.

"Dave, I've known your dad since we were kids. I'm telling you, your dad wouldn't hurt anyone."

"Then who killed Mr. Duggan?"

"Duggan had his fingers in a lot of dirty things, Dave. I don't know the details, but there's no shortage of candidates."

"What do the police think?"

"They're working on it."

"That doesn't do me or Sarah any good, does it? As long as my dad's the leading candidate."

"I'll get to the bottom of it, Dave. I promise. Your dad was innocent, and I won't let his son live with that stigma."

He smiled and thanked me, and I got up to leave.

"That's important to me, Mr. Proctor."

I nodded and patted his arm.

"Before you go. Mr. Proctor, what's a perc test?"

I looked at him curiously. I couldn't imagine where he'd even heard that term.

"A perc test is a test that land developers run to show how fast water drains from a property."

"Is it important?"

"Can be. If a property is not on a sewer line, you need a septic field for a new house. Can't put in a septic system unless the property percs."

"What's it mean if the property doesn't perc?"

"It means you can't develop it. Why, Dave?"

"It's something I heard Uncle Paul talking about. He said it would perc."

I wasn't expecting that at all.

"Perc?" I said. "What would perc?"

"I don't know."

"Who was Paul talking to?"

"I don't know. That's all I heard. Uncle Paul was on the phone. I remember because he seemed pretty excited about it."

"When was that?"

Dave thought a minute.

"Four or five days ago. After my mom died but before all this happened. I was in this room when the phone rang."

"What else did he say?"

"Not much. He put his hand over the mouthpiece and asked me to leave the room and I did."

"Did you hear anything else?"

He laughed.

"No, I didn't listen at the keyhole. Maybe I should have. Do you think it has anything to do with my property?"

"*Your* property?"

He flashed the indulgent smile of a parent dealing with a recalcitrant child.

"You sound like Uncle Paul. You know what I mean—the property he holds in trust for Sarah and me."

"Did you ask him about it?"

"Yeah. I asked him the same thing I asked you. He said it was nothing, just a detail that developers talk about."

"That's true. It is."

"Except that when I kept asking, he said it was none of my business. Why would he say that?"

"I don't know, Dave."

He turned his head toward the molding in the corner of the room. I could tell this whole thing made him uncomfortable and that he was not going to let it go.

"I was asking my uncle a general question about something that *is* my business. He could have told me.

Or he could have said he'd tell me another time. If it really wasn't any of my business, it would have been easy to tell me what it meant, don't you think?"

"Paul's under a lot of stress, Dave. I know you are, too. Maybe you need to give him some space."

"Giving him space is no problem. He takes me out for a drive just about every day, but other than that, I've hardly seen him since I've moved in."

"Okay. Anything else I can help you with?"

He studied his hands and looked up.

"I want to know who killed my dad."

A vision of Jimmie Flambeau popped up.

"And who killed Mr. Duggan."

"It wasn't your father," I said.

"I know that. But who?"

"I'm working on it, Dave. Along with everything else."

We said our good-byes and I told him to call me if he needed anything.

I walked to my car with Jimmie Flambeau on my mind.

Chapter Seventeen

Digging Deeper

I'd met Lori McIntire when she was dating Sully. I remembered she was a hydrologist, employed by the EPA. She was smart and savvy and not the type to be pushed around by Sully or anyone else. As I dialed up my memory, I recalled a woman who looked a lot like Heather, maybe even a little bit prettier. I could never figure what she saw in Sully unless she was the type who liked men as reclamation projects.

I tracked her down at the EPA's Crystal City office and called her there that day and the next morning. When two messages weren't returned, I let it drop, but the next afternoon, while shopping for groceries at the Safeway in Cherrydale, I ran into her in the frozen food aisle. I'm not sure I would have recognized her if she hadn't been on my mind, and it was the immediacy of the recollection that caused me to blurt out her name. It took her a moment to put a name to my face.

"Joth?"

"Joth Proctor."

"Joth Proctor. Right."

She studied my face carefully as she processed my unexpected appearance.

"This isn't a coincidence, is it?"

Lori's attitude toward style bordered on insouciance. She favored simple outfits, unadorned by jewelry, but she had a superb eye for color, a trim figure, and a grace and presence that pulled everything together. She was wearing a skirt with a tartan pattern running through it and a light blue turtleneck under a blue blazer.

"Actually, it is," I said.

My embarrassment must have been palpable. She didn't believe me for a second.

"This is about Sully."

I held my hands up as if to surrender.

"No," I said. "Actually, I just came in here for some groceries."

"Really?"

She made her exaggerated doubt quite clear.

"Really."

"I shop here at the same time every Thursday, Joth. I've never seen you here before. Ever."

"I don't buy a lot of groceries. I'm not much of a cook."

She surveyed the collection of TV dinners and frozen pizzas in my shopping cart.

"I heard what happened," she said. "The paper said he drowned. The police came to see me about it."

"Standard procedure, Lori. What did you tell them?"

"I had nothing to say. I hadn't seen him in a couple of weeks, and we'd been drifting apart before that. Still, I was pretty shaken up by it. He wasn't a bad sort, all in all. And there's the two kids."

She shuddered and let her thought go unfinished.

"It'll be tough for them," I said.

She nodded.

"You represented him in his disbarment, didn't you?"

"Yes."

She made a face as if she were reaching some internal conclusion.

"Okay, Joth. You didn't call to tell me Sully was dead."

I remembered there was a Starbucks in a recessed area at the front of the store. Taking a chance, I swung around and tossed my head in that direction.

"Do you have time for a cup of coffee?"

Lori studied my face again and I wondered if she saw me as a potential salvage project. A man can dream, even in the most awkward moment.

"Why not?" she said.

Despite his occasional disdain for the gender, Sully
always had an uncanny knack with females. He was reasonably handsome as these things go, but what he had
going for him was the reckless and vaguely dangerous
way he lived his life. While this seemed to make him attractive, it crossed my mind that it could also be what got
him into the ultimate trouble. Still, women had been intrigued by Sully. None of them seemed to hang around
very long, but that was the way he seemed to like it. I
figured he and Lori had lasted about four months together before their inevitable breakup.

Lori took a chair at a round table in the corner of the
coffee bar and I got us a couple of lattes. Leaning on the
bar as the barista filled the order, it occurred to me that
Lori wasn't as pretty as I remembered her. What she had
was a poise and unaffected animation that trumped any
limitations in her physical appearance. She radiated intelligence and a confident, open approach to life, which
was attractive. I returned with two steaming paper cups
and sat across from her.

"You live near here?" she said.

I smiled. She was still probing my coincidental appearance.

"It's the closest grocery store to my house, if that's
what you mean."

She stared at me, willing to be satisfied with the answer.

"Joth, are you going to tell me what happened to Sully?"

"It's not clear yet."

"It was an accident, wasn't it?"

She sounded hopeful, even though she knew better, but I humored her with an ambiguous answer.

"Nobody really knows what happened, Lori."

"How are the kids taking it?"

"It hit them pretty hard."

"The one I feel sorry for is Sarah. She's a good kid."

"You were close to her?"

"I was. I grew up in a broken home, so I was always keeping an eye on her. It's hard growing up without a mom."

I remembered seeing Lori at the hockey game with Sully not long after Holly's death.

"I'll bet Sully appreciated that."

"I'm not sure he even noticed, to tell you the truth."

She sighed as her thoughts dwelled on Sully's daughter.

"She's much more vulnerable than her brother, Dave."

"She's got a good support group."

"It'll take more than a good support group to get her through this."

Lori winced.

"Well, enough about me," she said. "You called me about something?"

"Yes, I hope you can help me. And help the kids."

"I'll try."

"You're a hydrologist as I recall?"

She nodded.

"What do you know about perc tests?"

"I know you need to make sure a property percs before you can develop it."

"Or subdivide it, correct?"

"Sure."

"You've done that before?"

"That's what I did before I went to work for the EPA."

I felt like I was qualifying an expert witness.

"You ever do any work on any of Sully's properties?"

"No," she said. "I'm sure he would have used a professional. His brother-in-law must have a contact."

"Not this time."

"Why not?"

I could see that she had an inkling of what I meant. I gave her a little nod, to let her know she was snooping.

"There's a little stress in the family," I said. "But that's to be expected under the circumstances, right? You may have noticed that."

"They've been at each other a little bit."

"About what?"

She laughed as if she'd said too much and her cheeks dimpled.

"But no, Joth, he didn't ask me about a perc test."

"Are they difficult to do?"

"No. You need some tools and a few hours on a dry day. And that's why you called me?"

For some reason, I gave her the truth.

"And I wanted to see how you were doing."

She smiled and her face dimpled again. It was really the only feature she had in common with Heather.

"Well, I'm glad you did."

Lori fiddled with her coffee cup though she hadn't tasted a drop.

"Tell me about Sarah," she said.

"According to Mary, she's doing all right. She's never alone and her girlfriends' mothers are spending time with her, making sure she always has someone to talk to."

I kept this kind of talk going for several minutes. I was making a lot of it up, but if Lori saw through me, she gave no indication.

"Let her know I'd be happy to do what I can for her," she said. "That's a tough assignment, Joth. Do you think you can handle it?"

I offered a thin smile.

"I'll tell her."

Sully had always been satisfied with superficial relationships, even with his wife. I wondered how long it had taken Lori to figure that out. Then, as if she'd read my thoughts, she told me something else.

"What happened with Holly really hurt him."

"I'm sure it did," I said.

I felt chastened for even venturing a foot into flirtatious territory.

Lori changed topics and we chatted for a time about her job and pollution in the Chesapeake Bay. By the time I finished my latte, her untouched cup must have been cold.

"Lori, I appreciate you taking the time," I said. "Especially since you don't drink coffee."

She stood up and smiled.

"Remember what I told you to tell Sarah, will you?"

I nodded.

"I hope I'll have the chance to report to you personally."

Chapter Eighteen

The Perc Test

Under the circumstances, Paul planned a quiet observance of Sully's passing, but the Dwyer brothers had other ideas. They donated the leftover liquor from Holly's wake to serve at the post-service brunch, which caused the crowd to quickly spill out the front door of the Saunders home.

I saw old friends I hadn't seen in years. The service also attracted the press and freelance photographers, all hoping to gather salacious details at the fringes of a double murder. Sympathy for the orphaned children was palpable, but so was a lingering suspicion that the man whose memory we were all honoring might be a killer. It seemed like half of Arlington showed up. Among those distinctly not in attendance, though, was Jimmie Flambeau.

I got there early, along with Paul and Mary Saunders, and stood with Dave and Sarah in the receiving line as they accepted condolences from a long assemblage of mostly sincere adults, many of whom claimed a close relationship with the family. That duty done, I found a group of cushioned metal chairs, where I sat with Dave and Sarah.

A few minutes later, Lori McIntire joined us, and we made small talk until we ran out of things to say. In time, others stepped up to assume the duty. As Lori and I got up and moved away, an idea occurred to me. I offered her a drink from the Dwyer brothers supply.

"Looks like you could use one," I said.

She bobbed her eyebrows in a gesture of self-recognition and agreed.

"What a day."

"It's rough," I said. "No way around it."

"You know, Sarah may be the reason I stuck with Sully as long as I did. That girl has a good soul."

"That's something I'm starting to feel is in short supply around here," I said.

I glanced slowly around the room to make my point.

"Joth, I hate the sense of suspicion that's hanging over everything here."

"I know," I said. "We just have to ride it out."

"Sully had his failings," said Lori, "we know that, but he was one of the good souls, too. I know he couldn't have killed anyone. Not even his worst enemy."

I wondered if Jimmie Flambeau agreed with her sentiment.

"I think you're right," I said. "And I think I can prove it."

"How?"

I decided to get right to the point.

"We talked about a perc test, Lori. Remember? Can I hire you to do one?"

"What's a perc test got to do with what happened to Sully?"

"Everything. Can I get you to do one?"

It was an odd proposition from a man she hardly knew, and she hesitated.

"It wouldn't be worth much," she said. "I'm no longer certified."

"I don't want to rely on it, and I don't necessarily need to. I just want to know if a property percs."

Lori was still suspicious, but also intrigued by the request.

"Is it your property?"

For a brief moment I considered lying to her but thought better of it.

"No."

"Whose is it?"

I glanced toward Sully's kids, who were backed into a corner by a mass of seemingly supportive adults. "As a matter of fact, it belongs to Dave and Sarah Sullivan."

She looked at the crowd and then at me. As she sucked her bottom lip between her teeth, I thought I saw her consider both my request and what might be behind it.

"You should have told me that in the first place, Joth. You know I'll need authorization from one of them."

"That won't be a problem."

"Anybody else know about this?"

"Definitely not. Tomorrow's Saturday. Could we do it then?"

"I don't see why not, as long as the weather cooperates."

"How long does it take?"

I really had no idea.

"A couple of hours."

We discussed what she'd need—a garden hose and a bucket, a posthole digger and a shovel.

"I can bring everything else we need," she said.

I wrote the address on the back of a business card and handed it to her.

"Can we meet out there around eight in the morning?"

"Are you going to have Dave there?"

"I've got a feeling he'll insist on it."

Lori looked at her watch and so did I.

"Okay, Joth, eight tomorrow."

"Thank you."

Before leaving, I pulled Dave aside and asked if he had time the following morning to spend a few hours with me. In the close proximity of so many people, I told him I wanted to take him hiking, but he didn't believe it. He looked into my face for a sign of what I intended, but I couldn't clarify, not yet. I held my gaze on him, as if to let him know this was serious and necessary. He agreed without hesitation, but not without a small rhetorical dig.

"Hiking, huh?"

"Yeah, Dave. Wear your old clothes."

I knew he sensed that I felt a duty to his father and that I was ready to act on it. As I walked out to my car, I felt the glow of that conviction. The Saunders house was crowded with people who were handing out platitudes like cheese and crackers and who would disappear from the lives of Sully's kids in a few hours. For me, it would be different. The next day I would test my hypothesis and the pieces would either come together, or they'd fall apart like a loose deck of cards.

I picked up Dave at 7:30 the next morning. Mary Saunders ushered me into the library, where I turned down an offer of coffee as we waited for Dave to come down.

"Paul around today?" I said.

She shook her head without looking at me.

"He's in D.C. again" she said.

I concluded that she was telling the truth as she knew it.

Before I could follow up, Dave rumbled down the stairs, wearing jeans and hiking boots. I told Mary I was taking him to hike Billy Goat Trail along the Maryland bank of the Potomac. He kissed his aunt's cheek, said good-bye and we walked out to my car.

"Where are we really going?" he said, as we pulled out onto Ridge Road.

"We're going to take a look at your property."

"To see if it percs?"

"To see if it percs."

He didn't say anything else, didn't question the purpose or the goal. He understood more than I would have given him credit for, and I was pleased.

We were early, but Lori was already there, reading *The Washington Post* in the front seat of her blue Mini Cooper. The morning was clear with a chill in the air when the wind gusted. She got out as I pulled up behind her.

After we shook hands, she turned to Dave.

"I understand this is now your property, Dave."

"That's right."

"Joth wants me to run a perc test. Now, I'm not certified, so you can't use the results in any kind of official site development plan."

"I understand, Lori. It's just kind of informal."

"Correct. Do I have your permission?"

"Absolutely."

Lori was dressed for the job and the brisk weather. She wore a light ski vest over a blue windbreaker, and her hair was pulled back under a navy blue knit cap. She took a canvas bag from the trunk of her car and peered up the driveway toward the backyard.

"Let's see what we've got."

I looked up and down the street. We were alone and unwatched. Dave and I followed Lori up the rise. We weren't doing anything illegal, but a sense of foreboding hung over me like a fog.

By that point, the police had completed the recovery of George Duggan's body and their investigation of the scene. The trail in the grass that led me to the back of the yard had been further trampled by the feet of curious neighbors and titillated kids, but the novelty had already worn thin. The hole had been filled in and leveled. Shreds of police tape dangled in the breeze from several trees, but otherwise the backyard had the appearance of a vacant lot that kids used to play touch football.

Lori scanned the yard like a general seeking high ground, and I sent Dave to the shed for the posthole digger I had seen there on my previous visit. He rejoined us carrying the heavy tool over his shoulder like a weapon. Lori ran her thumb along the steel jaw of the digger, flicking off clumps of caked mud.

She tilted her head curiously. I noticed a faint stain on the back side of the other blade. It looked like rust but could've been blood.

Lori turned to consider the factors before us.

"Ordinarily, I'd suggest we take borings in three locations," she said, "but if you just want a kind of big picture understanding, I could do it another way."

I answered for Dave and myself.

"That's what we're looking for."

Dave nodded.

I wanted to get in and out as soon as possible, on the off chance that Paul might come by, or maybe one of Jimmie Flambeau's friends.

"Where would it make sense to start?" Dave said.

"Depends on how you envision developing it. You need a septic field for each house you expect to put up. How many did you have in mind?"

Lori was looking at me, but Dave answered without hesitation.

"Three."

"All right."

She glanced about and pointed in three disparate directions.

"Probably there, there and there are the places you'd bore."

"But the results are likely to be the same in each one, right?"

"I would say so."

I steered her away from George Duggan's burial trench toward the center of the backyard. She walked purposefully in that direction, with Dave and me following, until she tripped over something. I grabbed her arm before she fell. She regained her balance and we looked for the object that had caught her toe. It was a hole in the ground not much wider than the circumference of a coffee can. The fringes of it were ragged, but it looked relatively fresh. She kicked at it.

"Any chance somebody's already done a perc test?" she said.

Dave waited for me to answer.

"Not that I know of," I said.

"Dave, did your dad ever talk about a perc test?"

"Definitely not."

Lori looked at Dave and then at me and nodded.

"Okay, let's do it," she said.

She stopped about twenty yards from the back edge of the yard. Reaching down for a broken branch, she used it to inscribe a rough circle about ten yards in diameter on the ground, and then bisected it twice in the form of an air-drawn X. She instructed Dave to dig five holes of varying depths along the axis of the holes. He lowered the posthole digger from his shoulder and started in.

"I'll need a hose," she said.

I saw a garden hose still attached to a faucet alongside the house. I found it unspooled and in a pile under a set of stairs leading up to the kitchen door. The hose was long enough to reach the boring site Lori had selected. I dragged it by the nozzle to the back of the yard.

Dave dug steadily with calm energy, like a man used to manual labor, moving from one spot along the axis to the next. Lori took a tape measure out of her bag and as Dave completed each hole, she squatted down to measure the depth. When Dave completed the last hole, she instructed him on which ones to make deeper and how much. Within forty-five minutes, Dave was dripping sweat, and we had five holes of differing depths between one and four feet.

As Dave adjusted the depth of the last hole, I approached Lori.

"What do you think?" I said.

She picked up a handful of the hard, red soil.

"I don't know. There's a lot of clay in this. Let's find out."

After checking her watch and making a note of the time in her notebook, she filled each of the holes with water from the hose.

"Now what?"

"Now we wait."

I found a trio of molded white plastic chairs in the back of the garage. We set them up on a granite slab of the back patio where the morning sun could warm us. Then we waited.

A few minutes of small talk led us back to the subject at hand when I asked Lori what she expected the test to show.

"Clay is a common component of the soil around here," she said, "and the more clay, the slower the property will drain. We're also close to Difficult Run, meaning we're probably on the edge of the water table, so I wouldn't be optimistic, Dave."

"Maybe that explains why this property has never been developed," I said.

"That's possible," she said.

She looked again at Dave like she was preparing him for bad news.

"But hang on to it for a few years, Dave. Once the sewer system gets out here, it won't make any difference."

"That's fine," Dave said, "if you can afford to wait."

Our conversation drifted into different channels. We exchanged a few comments about the weather before Lori delicately turned to the other issue on everyone's mind.

"What's the future hold for you and your sister, Dave?"

Dave discussed his prospects at UVA, where he planned to study political science.

"Sarah's got two more years up here, but Uncle Paul and Aunt Mary have always been good to her," he said. "She's the youngest of the cousins, and Aunt Mary's always had a soft spot for her."

He looked at his watch. His eyes darted out to where the perc test was almost complete.

"Course it would be a lot easier on everybody if we could develop this property."

In response to Dave, Lori looked at her watch and nodded. She had done her best to dampen our expectations, but if Dave started across the backyard in high hopes, these were quickly dashed. The pooled water in each hole glistened in the morning sun.

The property did not perc.

"This isn't an official test, Dave," she said, "so you don't have to report it to anyone. And who knows? Maybe another test on another part of the property will get you different result."

"What are the chances of that?" he said.

She put her hands on her hips and scanned the yard.

"It's a big property, so maybe you could find one buildable lot back here, but to be honest, no; I don't think the chances are very good. You're just going to have to hang on to it until the sewer comes in. Or maybe you can flip it to a developer who is better able to hold on to it until then."

Dave nodded. I could see him taking in the information.

"It's still not a bad thing, is it?" he said.

"A multi-acre lot in Arlington County, Virginia is a good thing," Lori said.

This may have been true, but it hadn't been good to anyone yet.

Chapter Nineteen

Unexpected

Heather appeared in my office without warning the next afternoon. She looked like she hadn't slept. I wondered if she'd heard about my amateur perc test and had come to ask questions. We passed a few conversational remarks, but she hadn't come to my office to make small talk.

"Have you talked to Paul?" she said.

Something about her manner put me on guard.

"I saw him at the funeral. That's all. It isn't like I'm in a hurry to talk to him."

"He's been keeping a low profile."

She was fishing for information, but I felt oddly diffident toward her.

"I don't have a client anymore, Heather. I can talk, if you're willing to be equally frank."

"That business with the banker, it checks out. Paul's trying to get a construction loan from Hamilton, the guy he took to the game."

"Fat chance. He hasn't got a property to build on."

"Hamilton says he has a line on one, but so far it's just talk."

"That's something Paul is very good at."

Heather took a long look at me before changing her tack. She was wearing a silk blouse with a prim ruffled collar under a blue jacket and looked as if she was ready for court. She opened up a leather portfolio and removed two slim documents, which she placed on my desk: autopsies for Duggan and Sully.

I picked up Duggan's and looked it over.

"You were right, blunt object."

I decided to push her and see which way she'd bend.

"You still figure Sully killed him?"

"You tell me what makes more sense?" she said.

"That's your job."

"You knew him better than anyone, Joth."

I leaned forward.

"You know he didn't. You've never believed that. You've got two unsolved murders on your desk, Heather."

"Maybe three if you count Holly."

"That's why you're here. You need help."

"That's right, Joth. And you knew all the players. Are you willing to help me?"

It was coming down to was how much I trusted Heather, and I knew the answer to that—more than anyone else I knew. Plus, she was a good prosecutor in a tough spot.

"Paul has an alibi," I said.

She nodded.

"A solid alibi," she said.

She took a long breath.

"It's bad luck that the security cameras in the hotel garage weren't working."

I'd caught on to that point from the beginning, but there was no changing the facts. I raised my eyebrows.

"And?"

Heather reached across my desk, grabbed Sully's autopsy with two fingers and pulled it back into both her hands.

"Sully drowned, Joth, just as we suspected. The autopsy shows that he died around midnight. Maybe, just maybe, Paul went to the game and drove back to Arlington after it was over. He could do that in half an hour. Less, even. Let's say he met with Sully. There was an argument, and he killed him. Then he drove back to the hotel to complete his alibi in the morning."

I'd made that drive after many a Nationals game and the timeframe worked. I thought it through coldly for a minute. Nothing about her idea shocked me.

"You think he planned to kill him all along? That's why he went to the game? To establish an alibi?"

Heather folded her arms and considered it.

"No. I don't," she said.

Her voice lowered to what sounded like a conspiratorial whisper.

"Maybe it was a coincidence."

"Or maybe the game alibi was his backup plan," I said. "Just in case things ended up going sideways."

"Maybe. If my idea is plausible."

"It's plausible, Heather, but that won't get you a conviction, even assuming he did what you suggest."

She leaned forward with her elbows on the desk.

"Here's what I want you to do, Joth. Let it slip to Paul that the security cameras actually were working and that I'm going to review the tapes."

I lurched back in my chair, stunned.

"A couple of unsolved murders really turns the screws, doesn't it?"

"It's not evidence and it won't be," she said. "Get your guy DP on this; can you do that? He's been known to do worse."

"Not for me," I said.

"You'll deny it came from you if anybody ever asks."

"Which I'll have to if I don't want to get myself caught up in Paul's conspiracy defense."

"It'll never come to that, Joth."

"So if anybody asks, I was just making it up? Really, Heather? Just to see what he'd say?"

She ignored my point.

"Let's assume it's like I said. If Paul thinks the security tapes will show him leaving and returning to the garage before and after the murder, you'll know it. I mean, you'll see a reaction."

"Why are you asking me to do this?"

I knew the answer, but I wanted to hear her say it.

"Because you're close to him, Joth. You can go to his house on the ruse of visiting Sully's kids. And you'll do it because you're close to me."

This bothered me, that Heather expected me to be a lackey for her, but it bothered me more that a part of me was willing to consider it.

I shook my head, but I didn't kick her out of my office, which is what I should have done.

"Heather, if you asked a cop to do this, you'd have all kinds of problems."

"You're not a cop. That's why I'm asking you."

I slumped back in my chair. I stared at Heather. This whole thing had shaken her to the core.

"If you think Paul killed Sully, then who killed Duggan?"

"Right now, everyone thinks it's Thomas Sullivan. Who's left?"

So that was the bait. Heather would get her convictions, and I'd clear the name of my friend and client.

"What's the motive?" I said. "Why would Paul kill Duggan?"

"There were a lot of people he owed money to," she said.

She offered that as an offhanded comment, but she didn't even try to back it up. We'd worn each other out. As she got up to leave, I told her I'd think about it.

Walking out to my car after work that evening, I heard a sound that caught my attention. As I turned, I saw Officer Kelleher walking purposefully toward me from across the parking lot. She started speaking before she came to a stop.

"I have bad news for you, Mr. Proctor."

"What's that?"

"I have a warrant for your arrest."

Something about her appearance didn't feel right.

"What's the charge?"

She glanced about. I already had. We were alone.

"Suspicion of conspiracy to abet murder."

"Since when do you arrest people for that?"

"We do today."

"Let me see the warrant."

"We'll get to that when we get there."

"Where's 'there'?"

"Mr. Proctor, we can do this the hard way or the easy way. Now get in the car. You're driving."

She unsnapped the flap of her holster, and I did as I was told.

"Where are we going?" I said, as we exited the lot.

"Sheraton National Hotel. You know where that is?"

"Yeah."

The biggest hotel in Arlington was located off Washington Boulevard, overlooking the National Cemetery. Kelleher sat with her body angled toward me.

"Just who are we going to see?" I said.

"You'll see when we get there."

She was silent the rest of the way, and I was glad it was a short drive.

We parked in the underground lot. As we took the elevator to the sixth floor, I felt sweat prickling in my armpits.

"This way," she said.

Kelleher nudged me down the hall. When we reached the end, she knocked on a door, which quickly opened into the living room of a suite. The lights were low, and the curtains were drawn. In the center of the room, a big man in a suit stood on each side of a round table. Jimmie Flambeau sat at the table.

"Sit down," he said.

He didn't look up as he spoke.

I did as I was told.

Flambeau held a deck of playing cards. He shuffled them and turned over the top card. Ace of hearts. He slid out the bottom card. Ace of spades. He shuffled them again. This time, the top card was the ace of spades with the ace of hearts on the bottom. He shuffled again.

"You gonna tell me what happened?" he said.

His voice was unexpectedly silky.

"What happened to who?" I said.

"I haven't got time to play games."

I looked at the two thugs and then at Flambeau.

"If you want to know who killed George Duggan, I have no idea."

"No?"

"No."

"Kelleher thinks you do."

I looked around, but she was gone.

"She was dating Sully, you know. She's not exactly objective in all this."

"She went out with him once. She didn't like him anymore than he liked her."

I blew out a breath.

"I don't know who killed Duggan, I said, "or who killed Sully, either."

Flambeau continued working through the cards, pulling face cards from the middle of the deck.

"Kelleher thinks Sully met up with Duggan to discuss developing the property. It didn't go well. Things happened. She also thinks Sully might have taken you with him."

"Why would I do that?"

"You were his lawyer. Sully owed you money. If he didn't develop the property, you weren't going to get paid. And as I understand it, you're not exactly flush."

"You really think I'd kill somebody over an unpaid legal bill?"

He seemed surprised by the question.

"Sure."

I mustered a tone of disgust.

"Do you also think I killed Sully?"

Flambeau shrugged and looked up from the cards.

"The two of you argued, tried to push responsibility for what happened to Duggan onto each other. Hot-blooded people have accidents."

I looked again at his two thugs.

"I didn't kill anybody."

He pointed the deck of cards at me like a weapon.

"Then do yourself a favor. Find out who did."

Flambeau was smart and careful. I knew he would not permit shots to be fired inside the Sheraton National Hotel.

"I don't think either of your goons can take me by himself," I said, "and if they want to try it together, there's going to be a helluva noisy scuffle."

It took him a moment to process my comment. Then he laughed and settled back in his chair.

"Is that so?"

He waved his deck of cards and the thugs moved away from the table. The tension dissipated. I looked around again for Kelleher.

"How am I supposed to get back?"

"There's a cabstand downstairs."

"Not very sporting of you," I said.

Flambeau laughed again.

"Are you interested in some action on the Caps, Mr. Proctor?"

"No, no thank you. UVA football, maybe."

"We can talk about that."

"Paul Saunders is an old teammate. He says I can get some kind of action on Virginia football based on season results."

Flambeau paused for a moment.

"He may be speaking of what they call block betting. On the same money you can get different odds on the team finishing with a winning record, going to a bowl and winning the ACC. I'm speaking hypothetically, of course."

"Of course. Can I get in on that?"

"Football? It's a little early for football. Can I interest you in the Nats? The Orioles, maybe?"

"No. I guess I'll wait until August and get back to you on the 'Hoos. Assuming we solve our little problem, of course."

He nodded and smiled again.

"Please thank Paul for mentioning my services," he said.

"Well, I know he feels bad about the money he owes you."

"Paul doesn't owe me a dime," he said. "Matter of fact, he paid off his bill and his sister's too, not long before her untimely death."

"Wow. I know he owed you that money for a long time."

Flambeau chuckled.

"Mr. Proctor, nobody owes me money for a long time."

I nodded.

"I hope you understand that."

"I do now," I said.

With nothing left to discuss, I took the elevator downstairs and went outside to the cabstand. I knew Flambeau had long tentacles, so I shouldn't have been surprised to find that they reached into the police force, but I never saw it coming with Kelleher.

Chapter Twenty

Paul Comes Home to Roost

As soon as I got home, I hopped in my car to take a drive. I needed to clear my head and figure out the things I didn't understand. Two hours later, as it began to grow dark, I ended up on Ridge Road. One thing I'd decided was that I wasn't willing to be a tool of the criminal prosecution system, but as I approached Paul's house, that conviction faded. The garage door was open, and Paul's car was gone. Something had brought me here and I needed to trust my instinct. I pulled into the driveway, shut off the car and knocked on the door. There had to be something revealing inside that house.

As Mary said hello, smells emerged from the kitchen.

"Oh, Joth," she said, "I was expecting Paul."

"He always bragged about your cooking. Now I see why."

The aroma of chicken, spinach and coconut filled the house.

"He hasn't eaten much of it lately."

"Spending a lot of time on that new project?"

"The D.C. project, yes."

"Where's Dave?"

"He's with Paul. Dave's expressed an interest in the business, so what's an uncle for, right? Especially now. Keep him occupied."

"That's important," I said.

No matter what Paul had or hadn't done, I wasn't worried about Dave's physical safety, but I was uncomfortable with the idea of them spending too much time together.

I followed Mary back to the kitchen and took a seat at the table.

"What time do you think they'll be back?"

"They're late already. Why don't you join us for dinner?"

I demurred and she turned to something else.

"Let me ask your advice about something, Joth. You know Dave's birthday is coming up in a couple of weeks, and we're not quite sure what to do. It's not exactly time for a big celebration."

The mention of Dave's birthday reminded me of the Brownie Bust a year earlier. Dave had escaped punishment because he was under-age. Then the significance of his birthday hit me.

"He's turning eighteen."

"Yes," she said. "It's not as big a deal as it used to be. But it still marks a move into manhood."

255

"I'm afraid he's already reached that milestone."

"Yes, the hard way."

My observation launched Mary into a monologue about the fragility of youth and losing a parent too early. I barely heard a word of it. When I snapped out of my own private reverie, she was asking me again if I'd stay to eat.

"Paul's birthday is in November," I said, "if I recall that right."

"Yes. November 18. That usually makes for a pretty crazy Thanksgiving."

I stood up.

"Thanks for the invitation for dinner, Mary, but I really can't. Tell them both I asked for them."

I thanked her again and left.

Just before Ridge Road merged with Route 395, I saw Paul's car coming in the opposite direction. Dave was in the passenger seat. I ignored them and drove home.

Then I called Heather.

I hadn't called her home number since the day before she got married. Her husband, Pete, answered. A government contractor in the defense industry, he was good with people and rarely at a loss for words, but he was clearly surprised to hear my name.

"Can I tell her what it's about?"

"Never mind. I just need to talk to her."

She came on a minute later.

"This better be important," she said. "I'm putting the kids to bed."

"Well, the kids are going to have to put themselves to bed tonight."

I heard surprise in her breathing as she took a seat.

"Heather, the day you found Sully you showed me his iPhone."

She'd wanted my help earlier, but she had no obligation to open up to me now, at least not on my terms, and she had some pretty good reasons not to.

"Yes," she said.

"His iPhone had an appointment with J-P and you assumed it was me. Now I know who it was."

I waited, but she waited longer. I glanced at my watch. It was just past eight o'clock.

"If you want to know what happened, meet me at Rock Spring Park in half an hour. Can you do that?" I said.

"I'm supposed to trust you on this?"

"That's one thing you've always known, Heather. You can trust me."

"All right," she said. "Half an hour."

***

It was a bright evening in early April. I parked at a dead end on the south side of the park and walked down the bike path to the wooden bridge that spanned a bend in the creek. The moon was a day short of full, illuminating the path, and a gentle breeze blew through the treetops. An asphalt path ran north and south into the neighborhoods beyond both sides of the park. A few house lights appeared from homes up on the rise.

Heather was about ten minutes late, arriving so quietly she was almost beside me before I noticed her presence.

"Lost in thought?" she said.

"A lot to think about." ——

Venus and Jupiter were bright in the sky, and the moonlight silhouetted her sharp features. I could feel her staring at me, evaluating me, wondering what I was up to.

"You know, Joth, you're asking a lot of me."

I was standing at the place where my closest friend had been murdered. That made me anxious as I tried to envision the scenario I was still mapping out in my head.

I leaned my back against the railing of the bridge. Heather stood across from me, arms folded, impatient and grim.

"Holly and Paul had a lot of things in common," I said. "For one, they both liked to bet on college football games."

"No secret there."

"Let's assume for a second that they both got behind with Jimmie Flambeau."

Her posture stiffened.

"Not a guy you want to owe."

"So what would Paul Saunders do in a situation like that?" I said. "Probably try to work his way out of the hole by gambling on hockey over the winter."

"And he just got in deeper."

I nodded.

"So he needed money. And Holly needed money, too."

Heather closed her eyes a second and then looked hard at me.

"So Flambeau kills Holly to make a point to Paul?"

I shook my head and waved her off. I'd seen enough of Jimmie Flambeau to realize that he was a man who didn't use overt violence to get what he wanted. Instead, he constructed intimidating tableaux, using psychology to scare people into complying.

"That was the wrong course we all got off on, Heather. Jimmie Flambeau wouldn't kill anybody over a few thousand dollars. It's not worth it for him. He doesn't need to kill people because he's got everyone in the county afraid he might."

Heather was waiting for more.

"Holly died from a lethal combination of alcohol and sedatives. She died the way she lived, just like Sully said, and nobody would have thought twice about it if Paul hadn't panicked."

"Panicked about what?"

"About losing the property. When Holly died, she was still married to Sully, and by law, the property passed to her husband. It was also the one asset her brother thought he could count on."

Heather thought that through.

"Paul pledged it to Flambeau?"

"Flambeau deals in cash, Heather. He reminded me of that last night when he took the trouble to try to intimidate me. In person. He also confirmed that Paul had paid off his debts to him."

"Flambeau had been pressuring him?"

"Of course. He may not be a killer, but nobody who owes money to Flambeau lives too comfortably. But when Flambeau backed off, Sully thought Holly was blackmailing him. Nothing else made sense in a mind that worked like Sully's."

"Which brings us back to how they paid off Flambeau."

"Exactly. Paul had one asset. Or at least he thought he did. Heather, who do we know who would lend a significant amount of money based on the promise to deliver a developable property?"

"A lot of developers might do that."

"Most of them would want to make sure you have good title. George Duggan had other ways to perfect his claims."

Heather unscrewed the cap of her water bottle and took a sip.

"So Duggan lends Paul the money to get Flambeau off his back," she said.

"Yeah, and before they can get Holly to finalize the transfer, she drops dead."

"And the property passes to Sully."

"Who knows a golden goose when he sees one."

Heather moved to my side of the bridge, folded her hands and leaned her forearms against the metal railing next to me. It was a lot to think about. After a few minutes she broke the silence.

"Joth, you think Sully knew about the deal?"

"I don't know. If he did, he would have wanted a big piece of it. He may have seen this as his chance to make life miserable for George Duggan. He certainly had reason to want to stick it to him."

"Or he may have just wanted to develop it himself."

"Either way, Paul's stuck. He made a deal with the devil and he can't deliver."

"What's he do then?" she said.

"What would you do? He shucks and jives; he tells Duggan he'll take care of Sully out of his end, and then he makes half promises to Duggan and he screams and yells at everybody. What do you think?"

"George Duggan is not a patient man."

"Right. So here's where it gets a little fuzzy." I said. "Paul needs to move it along and Duggan's asking questions about the development potential. Paul thinks the property percs because that's what Sully told him. He picks up Duggan at his property at Potomac Yards and takes him over to the family lot for a show of good faith. He's going to demonstrate that it's developable as a step in the process. I think if you go over to that property, you'll find several coffee-can sized holes throughout the backyard, in addition to the five that I dug Saturday morning. The spot where they found Duggan was much bigger than necessary to bury him. That's because they were testing it as a septic field."

I waited a beat before dropping the news.

"Well, Heather, the property doesn't perc."

"How do you know that?"

"Lori McIntire. Sully's former girlfriend. She's a hydrologist. She ran a perc test for me Saturday morning."

"So it's worthless?"

"It's far from worthless, but it's not worth a whole lot right now. So then there's an argument between Paul and Duggan. Paul loses his temper, or panics, and hits Duggan over the head with the posthole digger. He may not have meant to kill him, but he's just as dead as if he did."

"And he buries him right there."

I nodded and shook my head all at once.

"What else is he going to do with a dead body on his hands?" I said. "Paul buries Duggan right there."

Heather blew out a long breath.

"Have you told this to anybody?"

"Nope."

She fell into silence again for a moment.

"And Sully figured it out?"

"Maybe, but I doubt it. More likely, Paul realized he'd never be safe as long as Sully owned the property where Duggan's body was buried. Sully would want to develop it, just as Paul had. It would just be a matter of time before Sully walked the grounds and discovered the body."

"So Paul's just as desperate now as he was before."

"More so. You see? Before, it was just money. Now, it's murder."

I let that rest for a second. I couldn't believe I was saying these things out loud, much less feeling sure they were true.

"And there's one other thing, Heather. As soon as Sully's dead, Paul holds the property as the trustee for Sully's estate."

"Meaning his kids, who are the beneficiaries."

"Yeah, but Dave's about to turn eighteen. As soon as he does, the owners will be Paul, as trustee for Sarah, and Dave, in his new capacity as an adult."

"And then all bets are off."

I nodded.

"Dave would have to agree before Paul could do anything with the property."

Heather gathered her thoughts.

"Do you think Dave's in danger?" she said.

"No," I said. "Not yet, at least. Because Paul is in control of the situation as long as Dave is a minor."

"So he'd still own it as trustee for the kids."

"Sure. But then what happens? The estate gets the profits on the sale of the developed property. In the meantime, Paul hires himself as the engineer, hires his company as the developer, and charges exorbitant funds to develop it. At the end of the day, they'll realize a good sale price, but the fees that Paul charged to the estate will suck up a lot of it. That's his plan, Heather—to drain the estate."

"Piece of work."

She dropped her head and resumed her deep thought while I listened to the stream trickle below the bridge beneath our feet. In the silence, we heard the slow footsteps of a couple approaching. We waited and let them pass until their footsteps couldn't be heard.

"But the Nationals game," Heather said. "It all checked out."

"Sure. Paul went to the game. But as soon as he said good-bye to that banker, he drove back across the Potomac."

I was long past those details.

"Heather, can you show me where they found Sully?"

The creek ran in a northerly direction toward its ultimate junction with the Potomac River, a mile away. She pulled out a flashlight, stepped off the path and down to the grass bank on the south side of the creek. Bullfrogs and a whoosh of cars from out-of-sight roads broke the silence. As we walked downstream, Heather focused her light onto the near bank. She stopped where the light hit a jagged rock that reached out into the creek.

"Right about there, Joth. He got hung up right there on that rock."

I took the flashlight from her hand.

"Do they know how long Sully had been dead before they found him?"

"As near as they can tell, he'd been dead for six or seven hours."

"So around midnight?" I said. "But his phone was still working? Where did they find it?"

"Up by the bridge."

"Fell out in the struggle?"

She nodded.

"Makes sense."

I took a drink from Heather's water bottle.

"Here's what happened, Heather. Paul lured Sully here. The appointment said J-P. You figured that to be Joth Proctor, but Sully wasn't likely to agree to meet Paul anywhere unless I was involved."

"So J-P meant . . ."

"Joth and Paul. Get it?" I said. "Paul told Sully to meet the two of us here that night. That's why Sully came."

"And his plan was to kill him."

"I don't think it was. No. The baseball game, the hotel, the elaborate alibi—think about it. I assume Paul was considering the worse-case scenario, but the plan was still to try to persuade Sully."

"Persuade him to do what?"

I took Heather by the elbow and led her back to the bridge where they'd found Sully's phone. From here, another narrower path led beneath the trees and away from the park, into a neighborhood of comfortable homes fifty yards up the rise.

Popped up ramblers, tidy brick colonials and a pair of Arts-and-Crafts style homes were spaced well apart on a street without sidewalks or streetlights. A broad canopy of trees spread darkness over the area like a cloak.

I stopped where the path entered the neighborhood.

"You been up here before?"

"Once or twice," she said. "Kind of above my pay grade."

"Mine, too. Like I said, Heather, all Paul wanted was the property. Don't forget, he's cancelled his debt to Duggan. Once he owned the land, he could wait until the time was right and get rid of Duggan's body. Then he could flip the property and his problems are in the past."

"But Sully wouldn't go along with it."

I shrugged.

"He may have smelled a rat. He may just have been stubborn. Sully saw this property as a godsend because it was a source of funds to educate his kids, which is exactly what Holly would have wanted."

I peeked at Heather, who was listening closely.

"Sully could drive a hard bargain if he thought he had the advantage," she said.

"Precisely."

I stopped a second, just to take in how well we were working as a team.

Chapter Twenty-One

The Arts-and-Crafts House

Looming in the darkness, occupying a lot on the corner of the street, sat a two-story, Arts-and-Crafts style home. On its grassy front lawn, a "For Sale" sign, bearing the Belle Terra Properties LLC logo, was stuck into the ground.

Heather's head snapped up when I pointed it out. I nodded. We walked up the flagstone walkway to a wraparound porch. I opened the screen door and handed her the flashlight.

"This is the place Paul offered Sully. This was his final play."

The realtor's lock box on the door was secured with a four-cylinder combination dial. I remembered that Paul had casually given me the combination when trying to persuade me to talk Sully into the trade.

11. 18. His birthday, as his wife had reminded me.

I spun one-one-one-eight into the dial and the box opened. Inside was a brass key. Heather gasped and exhaled loudly, but she made no effort to stop me. She was about to commit a felony—Breaking and Entering—but she was as anxious as me to see if the last piece of the puzzle fit.

The key turned and clicked, and the door opened. I reached inside, threw a light switch and we stepped into a small faux marble foyer with a lamp hanging in the middle. Beyond it, a set of stairs ran up to the second floor.

"I suppose we have permission to be here if anyone asks?" she said.

I couldn't help grinning at her anxiety.

"I suppose."

In the foyer was an antique umbrella stand filled with cheap collectibles. A walking stick, a cane, a small American flag on a pole, and a Louisville Slugger. A few pieces of showroom furniture populated the living room to the left and the dining room to the right. It was full of flimsy, non-descript articles intended to help the place sell.

We walked quietly through the first floor, like the trespassers we were.

"Paul wanted Sully to take this place in return for deeding him the Saunders family property?" she said.

"That was the idea," I said. "Probably some money would have changed hands as well. I imagine they went back and forth on that, with Sully pushing for every extra dollar he could. The way Paul saw it, Sully was living at the sufferance of a friend, and he ought to be glad to have a decent home for his kids."

"But Sully was uh . . ."

"Sully was stubborn," I said.

"And then what?"

We were whispering. I didn't know why, but it seemed appropriate.

"Paul couldn't kill him down in the park. There'd be too much noise and a strolling neighbor or two could walk through any time. But up here, it's different. Paul tells Sully he wants to show him the house and makes his final pitch to him here. Maybe he loses his famous temper, or maybe it's what he planned all along."

We both knew what we were looking for—signs of a struggle, overturned furniture, curtains pulled to the floor—anything, but the place was pristine. We completed a circle of the first floor and neither of us had noticed anything askew. Then Heather's head suddenly swiveled toward me.

"But Joth, he drowned."

"Right."

As if a light bulb went off, Heather started up the stairs and I followed. There was a full bath at the top of the landing. She switched on the light and examined it like she was searching for a mislaid jewel. She had the scent now. But the bathroom was as clean and presentable as the first floor, nothing out of order.

"So where did he kill him?" she said.

We moved down the hall into the master suite. Heather pushed open the door to the bathroom and flipped on the light.

"Here," she said.

The master bathroom was clean and tidy, but the arm of a towel rack had broken off and hung loosely. She checked the plaster where it had come loose, and we saw paint chips that must have flaked away. She grabbed my arm and pointed.

"He drowned him in the bathtub."

Next to the tub, the toilet paper holder had been knocked askew. A little nudge and it fell away, revealing duct tape that had been used for a temporary fix.

We stared at each other a second.

"Maybe they discussed it down at the bridge," Heather said, working through the rest of the scenario herself.

"But Paul would have set this up beforehand."

I nodded, encouraging her to continue.

"He had to. Probably the tub was already full. He made his last pitch. Sully said no. Wouldn't budge. Paul overpowered him and drowned him."

She sat on the edge of the tub and looked out the window.

"The moon's almost full tonight. Two weeks ago, it would have been moonless, and if Paul slipped out the back door, he would have been under the trees and out of sight, all the way down to the bridge."

I agreed.

"Paul's a big guy, much bigger than Sully. He carries him down and puts him in the stream. That couldn't have taken ten minutes, and nobody sees him. In his rush to get it done, he didn't notice when the phone fell from Sully's pocket."

"Yeah, and then the alibi he was hoping he wouldn't have to use comes back into play. He drives back to D.C. and goes to sleep in the hotel."

Heather folded her arms across her chest. Crow's feet formed like a perfect puzzle between her eyebrows as she channeled her thoughts.

"So he killed his brother-in-law," she said. "Over what?"

"Money. That's the usual reason."

A familiar voice came from behind us. We both turned to face Paul Saunders, standing in the bathroom doorway. In his gloved right hand, he held a revolver.

Heather glared, and he lifted the gun.

"Put that down, Paul."

His eyes were cold and remorseless.

"Be careful, both of you," he said. "It might go off. A lot of people get nervous when they find trespassers in their house."

I reached for Heather's arm in an attempt to pull her behind me, but she shrugged my hand away. Crime was her business and she gritted her teeth.

"Nobody would believe that, Paul."

He smiled. Beads of sweat collected at his temples. He was as anxious as I was.

"I'll tell you what they would believe," he said. "You two were rekindling your affair after all these years and using my house to do it."

"You're insane."

"Joth insists you leave your husband. You say no. Murder-suicide."

"Suspicion already rests on you for two murders," Heather said. "You can't get away with two more."

He returned Heather's calm stare.

"Really?" he said. You've been telling everyone that Sully killed Duggan and that George's friends avenged him. That story still works, you know."

Paul's eyes narrowed. He was speaking crisply, sure of his story, and waving the gun around to make his points.

"That story won't cover up any of this," I said.

"Sure it will."

He gestured at me with the revolver in his hand.

"You recognize this, Joth? Sure you do. This is your gun."

I recognized it. A .38 Diamondback, straight from my living room.

"Last time I was at your house, I knocked over a Jefferson Cup with a key in it. You were good enough to point out the gun case that it went to. Remember? So I borrowed it.

I stared at him. He laughed.

You see," he said, "it always helps to have somebody else's gun. Now let's go."

Heather stood up slowly and carefully from the edge of the tub, her boldness melting away.

"Where, Paul?"

"Master bedroom would be a good place."

"For what?"

Heather could barely put one foot in front of the other. I put a hand on her arm to steady her.

"No one's going to believe this, Paul."

"You believe it, don't you, Heather?"

I took a step forward toward the master bedroom.

"You can't fix this one, either, Joth."

Paul took one backward step into the bedroom and was about to take another when a pale, yellow flash of varnished Northern White Ash whipped through the air and struck him behind the ear. He went down in a heap at my feet and I stepped around him.

Quick as a cat, Heather kicked the gun away and gathered it up in both hands. With a moan, Paul slowly rolled into a ball against the side of the tub, where he held his bleeding head in his hands.

I stared at the doorway.

Dave Sullivan stepped into the bathroom, slapping the head of a Louisville Slugger into his palm, as if he just hit a game-winning home run. He would have hit Paul again, probably would have killed him, if I hadn't grabbed his arm and steadied him. I felt his bicep flex and then relax. He backed away.

I tried to take the gun from Heather, but she reminded me that she was the resident law enforcement official.

"Call 911," she said.

I pushed Dave into the bedroom and did as she instructed, reporting the circumstances to the dispatcher. By the time I completed the call, Paul was sitting up against the side of the tub. Dave had given him a good bash. He was conscious, but in a lot of pain.

"You've got nothing on me," he said.

"The hell we don't," I said.

Heather had a more sensible reply.

"Then what's this all about?"

"What are you doing in my house?"

Paul raised a feeble hand and pointed a finger at me.

"When the alarm sounded, I came to protect my property."

"What about that murder-suicide thing?" I said.

"I don't know what you're talking about."

"Except that I heard it too," said Dave.

Paul fell into a pained, sullen silence. The story stuck to him like glue. We were right, and he knew it.

The next sound I heard was a police siren. Three officers in commando sweaters and bulletproof vests hurried upstairs with guns drawn. They were startled to see Heather Burke staring right back at them. But they were used to deferring to her at crime scenes and did so without question.

Heather regained her composure with remarkable speed. Responding to a few crisp directives from her, one of the officers read Paul his rights as another cuffed him.

"Virginia Hospital Center," she said. "Get moving."

She jerked her head toward the street. Paul went with the officers, of course, but not without a struggle, cursing profanely until the downstairs door closed behind him.

I made a beeline for Heather's water bottle, draining it like a last swig of cheap whiskey on a Saturday night.

"Here's to you, Sully."

Chapter Twenty-Two

On the Plaza

Two days after Paul Saunders's arrest, my former teammate pled not guilty to a pair of homicides, two counts of attempted murder, one count of grand larceny and a weapons violation. He was denied bail, remanded to the custody of the sheriff, and incarcerated in the Arlington County jail.

Heather recused herself right away from the case, and her chief deputy issued an immediate no-contact order between Heather, Dave and me. This was to ensure that the police could collect unvarnished facts, and that our testimony would not be compared. We each gave separate formal statements before a court reporter and attested to their veracity.

Once that was done, we resumed our lives as best we could, waiting for the day when Paul Saunders would face a jury or plead guilty to murder.

Since the coast was now clear, Heather, Dave and I met at the fountain on Courthouse Plaza. I got there first and took a seat on one of the broad, granite steps. It was a warm day, and a gentle breeze rustled the first cherry blossoms of the season. Behind me, the fountain gushed in a stream of white foam and water that flowed down to the basin where I sat. The froth that sprayed down on me in the breeze was refreshing, like the first drops of a sun shower.

I welcomed any sign of optimism.

When Dave showed up, I stood and hugged him. He was a tough-minded kid. He'd been able to process what had happened and seemed to have accepted his lot on an intellectual level, but I knew it would be a while before he smiled again.

He explained that he and his sister had been removed from the Saunders home and were living in a local motel. I offered him my spare bedroom, at least until college began in the late summer, but Dave had already booked a summer of activities to keep him busy and out of town. He didn't know yet where Sarah would end up.

Before I could respond, we noticed Heather coming down the plaza. As soon as she saw us, she broke into a trot. Dave and I stood up as Heather threw an arm around each of our shoulders and hugged us both.

It didn't take long for the conversation to turn to Paul Saunders.

Heather wouldn't try the case because she'd be a witness, if it came to that. As a result, she was less circumspect than usual.

"I figure he has about a ten percent chance to beat either of the murder charges."

She looked at me, and I nodded in agreement. On paper, at least, there was reasonable doubt, but the jurors would figure it out.

"They're both capital charges," she said. "If Paul goes to trial on either one and loses, he's looking at the death penalty. My guess is, he'll take a plea to life in prison. Would that be okay with you, Dave?"

I looked at my godson. He may not have expected the question in that moment, and didn't appear ready to say anything out loud, but I could tell he'd already thought about it. His face tightened, then relaxed, and he looked at both of us before speaking.

"I want to get this behind me," he said. "And Sarah, too. We've seen enough death for a while."

I hadn't spoken to Dave since the night he rescued us. I wanted to know how he ended up at the house, but with the gag order in place, this was my first chance to find out.

"Dave, now I can finally ask you," I said. "What brought you there?"

He smiled.

Heather leaned in to make sure she didn't miss a word.

"Paul had a security system in place at the house. We were in the library, playing cards, when the alarm went off. He walked over to check it out. He shut it off and started pacing. It was like he suddenly forgot all about me and went into some kind of trance or something. I'll never forget his face, all red with his eyes bulging out. When Aunt Mary came in the room, he pushed right past her and headed for the door. Didn't say a thing. When she asked where he was going, he just said, 'the rental.' I'd been going on the rounds with Paul for a while. It didn't take me long to figure out what he meant and where it was located. Something just didn't sit right about any of it, so I followed him."

"In your dad's car?"

"It's my car now."

I nodded.

"What didn't sit right?" said Heather.

"Uncle Paul's whole story. He doesn't know a base-ball from a cantaloupe. He's a lacrosse guy. Why would he take a banker to a baseball game?"

"Business," I said. "He was working the guy."

"He went to the game," Heather said. "It checked out."

"He may have gone to that game," Dave said, "but I bet he can't tell you who pitched. If I was trying to develop a business relationship, I'd invite the guy to do something I know a little bit about."

I grinned. The apple hadn't fallen far from the tree. I could see that the business instincts that Dave had inherited from Sully would serve him well in the future.

"Uncle Paul was courting that banker to make it all look good. The whole scheme. He was ducking everybody else. That's why he was gone so much. Even Aunt Mary noticed. And now we know why."

"She told me he was in D.C. a lot recently," I said, "and that he spent a lot of time with you."

"He did," said Dave. "Almost every day he'd take me for a drive. He took me around to show me properties he said he had options on or plans to buy and develop. That's how I knew where the rental was. But mostly he'd talk about the family property. He said he wanted to teach me the business and strengthen our relationship, but it sounded pretty thin to me."

Dave looked at me and Heather.

"I think he liked to take me for drives because he could ask me questions without having to look me in the eye."

"What kind of questions?" said Heather.

"What I thought happened to dad, what I thought you two thought, what I thought about the family property. Things like that. He wanted to know how much I knew

or suspected. And how flexible I'd be on the family property once I turned eighteen."

"You'll own it in a few days," I said.

"Yeah, happy birthday to me," Dave said.

He sounded cynical but shrugged it off just as fast.

"I'll own it half on my own and half in trust for my
sister, right? Isn't that how it works?"

"That's how it works," I said.

"Okay. Well, I've got life insurance money to put us
through college, so I can afford to hold onto it. Maybe
you'd be the trustee for Sarah, Mr. Proctor. She'll need a
guardian, too."

The thought of that responsibility chilled me a little.
I wasn't sure it would be a good idea for either one of us.

"You'll be eighteen, Dave," I said.

"Maybe so, but I'm not in a position to take that on.
I'll be in college."

I nodded.

Dave had more sense than most kids his age.

"I'll make sure it's taken care of, Dave."

He smiled. He was still a high school kid, as he reminded me when he stood up and told us he had lacrosse
practice. I shook his hand and so did Heather. We
watched him walk under a large, white clock with black
Roman numerals mounted in the archway above the en-
trance to the plaza.

Then he strode off—a big, confident young man stepping into a bright future.

"He'll be all right," I said.

"Where are they going to live?" Heather said. "He and his sister?"

I told her Dave's plans.

"Sarah?"

I didn't reply and watched Heather put her chin in her hand.

"I'm not worried about Dave, Heather. It's Sarah. She could end up being the big loser in all this."

"You're right," she said. "As far as I can tell, I don't think she'll be too comfortable staying with her Aunt Mary."

"No," I said. "You're right. That's why I'll take it on. I'll be her guardian. I guess I could take her in my place."

"That would be a little awkward, don't you think? A man your age living with an unrelated high school girl."

I picked up a pebble and tossed it.

"Yeah, Heather, good point. You got a better idea?"

"Just happens that I do," she said. "And I've already spoken to her."

"Her?"

"Joth, think. Who do we know who knows Sarah, cares about her, and has the resources to help her?"

She waited.

"The only person I can think of is Lori McIntire."

Heather looked at me and smiled.

"For real?" I said. "You already set that up?"

She nodded.

"You haven't changed," I said.

Heather shrugged.

"No, really."

"Yeah, maybe," she said, "and maybe you should take me out for lunch today."

I smiled.

I wondered how long my good luck would last.

Coming Soon!

Friend of a Friend

Book 2

A Joth Proctor Fixer Mystery

by

James V. Irving

Proctor reluctantly agrees to represent Frank "Half Track" Racker, a friend of a friend, former all-American lacrosse player, and a financial advisor by profession. His legal problem quickly mushrooms into a series of shady cases, which challenge Proctor's skills, complicate his personal relationships, and put his livelihood at risk...

For more information

visit: www.SpeakingVolumes.us

Coming Soon!

OUT OF ORDER
by
BONNIE MacDOUGAL

Everyone has something to hide.

A successful career. A charismatic new husband. A
bright, limitless future. Philadelphia lawyer Campbell
Smith seems to have it all. But in Bonnie MacDougal's
powerful novel of suspense, beneath the thin surface of
tranquility and realized dreams, dark events threaten to
throw Cam Smith's neatly arranged life profoundly—and
perilously—Out of Order…

For more information
visit: www.SpeakingVolumes.us

Sign up for free and bargain books

Join the Speaking Volumes mailing list

Text

ILOVEBOOKS

to 22828 to get started.

CPSIA information can be obtained
at www.ICGtesting.com
Printed in the USA
HW101544080622
803LV00004B/34